"You will pay. But not with money."

Cressy swallowed. "You mean—in spite of everything—you're going to marry me?"

Draco's laugh was harsh. "No, not marriage, my sweet. I will not be caught again. This time I'm offering a less formal arrangement."

"You're saying that if I—sleep with you— you won't enforce my father's debts. Draco, if you loved me, you wouldn't..."

"I said that I wanted you, Cressida *mou*. I did not mention love."

GREEK TYCOONS

**They're the men who have everything—
except a bride....**

Wealth, power, charm—what else could a
heart-stoppingly handsome tycoon need?
In the GREEK TYCOONS miniseries you
have already been introduced to some
gorgeous Greek multimillionaires who are
in need of wives.

Now it's the turn of favorite
Harlequin Presents® author Sara Craven,
with her passionate and compelling romance
THE TYCOON'S MISTRESS

This tycoon has met his match and he's decided
he *has* to have her...*whatever* that takes!

Sara Craven

THE TYCOON'S MISTRESS

GREEK
TYCOONS

HARLEQUIN®

TORONTO • NEW YORK • LONDON
AMSTERDAM • PARIS • SYDNEY • HAMBURG
STOCKHOLM • ATHENS • TOKYO • MILAN • MADRID
PRAGUE • WARSAW • BUDAPEST • AUCKLAND

ISBN 0-373-12192-X

THE TYCOON'S MISTRESS

First North American Publication 2001.

CHAPTER ONE

CRESSIDA FIELDING turned her Fiat between the two stone pillars and drummed it up the long, curving drive to the house.

She brought the car to a halt on the wide gravel sweep outside the main entrance and sat for a moment, her hands still tensely gripping the steering wheel, staring up at the house.

The journey from the hospital had seemed endless, through all the narrow, winding lanes with the glare of the evening sun in her eyes, but she'd have gladly faced it again rather than the situation that now awaited her.

Her mind was still full of the image of her father in the intensive care unit, his skin grey under the bright lights and his bulky body strangely shrunken.

Lips tightening, Cressida shook herself mentally. She was not going to think like that. Her father's heart attack had been severe, but he was now making good progress. And when his condition was sufficiently stable, the surgeons would operate. And he would be fine again—in health at least.

And if it was up to her to ensure that he had a life to come back to, then—so be it.

With a sudden lift of the heart, she noticed her uncle's Range Rover was parked by the rhododendrons. At least she wasn't going to be alone.

As she went up the short flight of steps the front door opened to reveal the anxious figure of the housekeeper.

'Oh, Miss Cressy.' The older woman's relief was obvious. 'You're here at last.'

'Yes, Berry, dear.' Cressida put a comforting hand on Mrs Berryman's arm. 'I'm back.' She paused in the hall, looking round at the closed doors. She drew a deep breath. 'Is Sir Robert in the drawing room?'

'Yes, Miss Cressy. And Lady Kenny's with him. A tower of strength he's been. I don't know what I'd have done without them.' She paused. 'Can I bring you anything?'

'Some coffee, perhaps—and a few sandwiches, please. I couldn't eat on the plane.'

She watched Berry hurry away, then, with a sigh, walked across the hall. For a moment she halted, staring at herself in the big mirror which hung above the pretty crescent-shaped antique table.

She was a cool lady. Her boss said it with admiration, her friends with rueful smiles, and would-be lovers with exasperation bordering on hostility.

It was a persona she'd carefully and deliberately constructed. That she believed in.

But tonight there were cracks in the façade. Shadows of strain under the long-lashed grey-green eyes. Lines of tension tautening the self-contained mouth and emphasising the classic cheekbones.

It was the first time she'd had the chance to take a good look at herself, and the emotional roller-coaster of the past few weeks had left its mark.

Her clothes were creased from travel, and her pale blonde hair seemed to be sticking to her scalp, she thought, grimacing as she ran her fingers through it. She stopped for one deep, calming breath, then went into the drawing room.

She halted for a moment, assimilating with shock the

over-stuffed sofas, with their heavy brocade covers, and matching drapes, which managed to be expensive and charmless at the same time—all new since her last visit.

The lovely old Persian rugs had been replaced by a white fitted carpet, and there were gilt and crystal chandeliers instead of the graceful lamps she remembered, and mirrors everywhere.

It all looked like a stage setting, which had probably been exactly the intention, with Eloise playing the leading part—the nearest she'd ever come to it in her entire career. Only she'd quit before the end of the run…

Sir Robert, perched uneasily on the edge of a chair amid all this splendour, sprang to his feet with open relief when he saw Cressida.

'My dear child. This is a bad business.' He hugged her awkwardly. 'I still can't believe it.'

'Nor can I.' Cressida shook her head as she bent to kiss her aunt. 'Has there been any word from Eloise?'

'None,' Sir Robert said shortly. 'And we shouldn't expect any. She practically ransacked the house before she left.' He frowned. 'Berry says she's taken all your mother's jewellery, my dear.'

'Dad gave it to her when they were married,' Cressida reminded him evenly. 'She was entitled. And as least we're rid of her.'

'But at a terrible price.' Sir Robert pursed his lips. 'Of course, I could never understand what James saw in her.'

'Which makes you quite unique, darling,' his wife told him drily, drawing Cressida down to sit beside her.

'Eloise was a very beautiful, very sexy young woman and she took my unfortunate brother by storm. He was besotted by her from the moment they met, and probably still is.'

'Good God, Barbara, she's ruined him—she and her—paramour.'

'That's the trouble with love,' Cressida said slowly. 'It blinds you—drives you crazy...'

I never understood before, she thought painfully. But I do now. Oh, God, I do now...

She pulled herself together and looked at her uncle. 'Is it really true? It's not just some terrible mistake?'

Sir Robert shook his head soberly. 'The mistake was your father's, I'm afraid. It seems he met this Caravas man when he and Eloise were in Barbados two years ago. He claimed to be a financial adviser, produced adequate credentials, and gave them a few bits of advice which were perfectly sound.' His mouth tightened. 'I think they call it salting the mine.'

'When did he first mention the Paradise Grove development?'

'Several months later,' her uncle said grimly. 'They happened to run into him at the ballet, it seems, except there was nothing random about the encounter. There were a couple of other meetings—dinner, an evening at Glyndebourne which he paid for—then he started talking about this exclusive hotel and leisure complex, and what an investment opportunity it was. He said it would make them millionaires many times over, but only a really high investment would bring a high return.'

Cressy drew a painful breath. 'So Dad put all his money into it? And remortgaged this house? Everything?'

Sir Robert's nod was heavy. 'If only James had told me what he was planning, I might have been able to talk him out of it. But by the time I found out what was troubling him, it was too late.'

'And, of course, it was a sting.' Cressy looked down

at her clasped hands. Her voice was level. 'Paradise Grove was a mangrove swamp in the middle of nowhere. No one was ever going to build anything there.'

'Yes. But it was clever. I've seen the plans—the architects' drawings—the documentation. Including the apparent government licences and permissions. It all looked very professional—very official.'

'Like all the best confidence tricks.' Cressy shook her head. 'And the clever Mr Caravas? When did he and Eloise get together?'

'I imagine quite early on. There's no doubt she pushed James into the scheme for all she was worth. And now she and Caravas have completely vanished. The police say that they'll have new identities and the money safely laundered into a numbered account somewhere. Their plans were carefully made.' He paused. 'Your father wasn't the only victim, of course.'

Cressy closed her eyes. She said, 'How on earth could Dad have taken such an appalling risk?'

Sir Robert cleared his throat. 'My dear, he was always a gambler. That was part of his success in business. But he'd had some stockmarket losses, and—other problems. He saw it as a way of ensuring his long-term security in one big deal. He's never taken kindly to retirement. He wanted to be a key player again.' He paused. 'Quite apart from the personal pressure.'

'Yes,' Cressida said bitterly. 'And now I have to see if there's anything that can be saved from this ghastly mess.' She looked around her. 'I suppose this house will have to go.'

'It seems so,' Barbara Kenny said unhappily. 'I doubt if James will have much left apart from his company pension.'

Cressy nodded, her face set. 'I've brought my laptop

down with me. Tomorrow I'll start looking—finding out how bad things really are.'

There was a tap on the door and Mrs Berryman came in with a tray. The scent of the coffee, and the sight of the pile of ham sandwiches, the plate of home-made shortbread and the rich Dundee cake accompanying them, reminded Cressy how long it was since she'd eaten.

She said warmly, 'Berry—that looks wonderful.'

'You look as if you need it.' The housekeeper's glance was searching as well as affectionate. 'You've lost weight.'

'Berry's right,' her aunt commented when they were alone again. 'You are thinner.'

Cressy was pouring coffee. 'I expect it's an illusion created by my Greek suntan. Although I did do a lot of walking while I was out there.' *And swimming. And dancing...*

'My dear, I'm so sorry that your holiday had to be interrupted like this,' Sir Robert said heavily. 'But I felt you had to be told—even before James collapsed.'

Cressy forced a smile. 'It was time I came back anyway.' Her mouth tightened. 'You can have—too much of a good thing.' She handed round the coffee and offered the plate of sandwiches. 'I'd have been here sooner, but of course it's the height of the holiday season and I couldn't get a flight straight away. I had to spend a whole day in Athens.'

It had been a nervy, edgy day—a day she'd spent looking behind her constantly to see if she was being followed. She'd joined a guided tour of the Acropolis, mingled with the crowds in the Plaka, done everything she could to lose herself in sheer numbers. And all the time she had been waiting—waiting for a hand on her shoulder—a voice speaking her name…

'Cressy, I worry about you,' Lady Kenny said forthrightly. 'You don't have enough fun. You shouldn't have your nose stuck to a computer screen all the time, solving other people's tax problems. You should find yourself a young man. Start living.'

'I like my job,' Cressy said mildly. 'And if by "living" you mean I should be swept away by some grand passion, I think we've seen enough of that in this family.' Her face hardened. 'Watching my father make a fool of himself over someone as worthless as Eloise taught me a valuable lesson. I've seen at first hand the damage that sex can do.'

'He was lonely for a long time,' her aunt said quietly. 'Your mother's death hit him hard. And Eloise was very clever—very manipulative. Don't be too hard on him, darling.'

'No,' Cressy said with sudden bitterness. 'I've no right to judge anybody. It's all too easy to succumb to that particular madness.' *As I know now.*

For a moment she saw a cobalt sea and a strip of dazzling white sand, fringed with rocks as bleached as bones. And she saw dark eyes with laughter in their depths that glittered at her from a face of sculpted bronze. Laughter, she thought, that could, in an instant, change to hunger…

Suddenly breathless, she drove that particular image back into the recesses of her memory and slammed the door on it.

She would not think of him, she told herself savagely. She could not…

She saw her aunt and uncle looking faintly surprised, and went on hurriedly, 'But I shouldn't have let my dislike of Eloise keep me away. Maybe if I'd been around I could have done something. Persuaded Dad, somehow, that Paradise Grove was a scam. And he might not be in Intensive Care now,' she added, biting her lip hard as tears stung her eyes.

Sir Robert patted her shoulder. 'Cressy, you're the last person who could possibly be blamed for all this. And the doctor told me that James's heart attack could have happened at any time. He had warning signs over a year ago. But he wanted to pretend he was still young and strong.'

'For Eloise,' Cressy said bitterly. 'Oh, why did he have to meet her?'

Lady Kenny said gently, 'Sometimes fate works in strange ways, Cressy.' She paused. 'I've prepared a room at our house if you'd like to come back and stay. You shouldn't be on your own at a time like this.'

'It's sweet of you,' Cressy said gratefully. 'But I must remain here. I told the hospital it was where I'd be. And I shan't be alone with Berry to look after me.'

'Ah, yes.' Sir Robert sighed. 'I'm afraid Berry may be another casualty of this debacle.'

'Oh, surely not,' Cressy said in swift distress. 'She's always been part of this family.' One change that Eloise had not been allowed to make, she added silently.

Sir Robert finished his coffee and put down his cup. 'My dear.' His tone was sober. 'I think you must accept that nothing is ever going to be the same again.'

He was right, Cressy thought as she stood on the steps an hour later, waving her aunt and uncle an approximation of a cheerful goodbye.

Everything had changed quite momentously. Beginning with herself.

She shook herself mentally as she went back into the house.

She had to forget about those days of golden, sunlit madness on Myros, and how near she too had come to making a disastrous mistake.

That urgent summons back to England, although devastating, had been in another way a lifeline, dragging her back to reality. Waking her from the dangerous seductive dream which had enthralled her and could have led her to total ruin.

A holiday romance—that was all it had been. As trivial and tawdry as these things always were, with a handsome Greek on one side and a bored tourist on the other. Just for a while she'd allowed herself to indulge a risky fantasy, and then real life had intervened, just in time, returning her to sanity.

For a moment she found herself wondering what would have happened if her uncle's message had not been waiting at the hotel. If she'd actually called Draco's bluff and gone back to Myros...

She stopped herself right there. Speculation of that kind was forbidden territory now. Myros, and all that had happened there, was in the past, where it belonged. A memory that one day, in years to come, she might take out, dust down and smile over.

The memory of desire and being desired...

But not now. And maybe not ever, she thought, straightening her shoulders.

Now she had to look to the immediate future, and its problems. She'd have an early night, and tomorrow she would start to sift through the wreckage, see if anything could be salvaged.

And tonight, she told herself with determination, she would sleep without dreaming.

* * *

But that was more easily said than done. Cressida's night was restless. She woke several times, her body damp with perspiration, haunted by images that left no trace in her memory. Nothing that she could rationalise, and then dismiss.

Perhaps it was simply coming back to this house, where she'd been a stranger for so long, and finding herself in her old room again. The past playing tricks with her unconscious mind.

At least this room hadn't undergone the high-priced makeover inflicted on the rest of the house.

Eloise had been determined to erase every trace of her predecessor, Cressy thought, more with sorrow than with anger. And no expense had been spared in the process—which could explain how James Fielding might have found himself strapped for cash and been tempted to recklessness.

Although, in fairness, this wasn't the first time her father had sailed close to the wind. Only this time his instinct for disaster seemed to have deserted him.

But that, she thought, can happen to the best of us.

She pushed back the covers and got out of bed, wandering across to the window. Light was just beginning to stain the eastern sky, and the cool morning air made her shiver in her thin cotton nightgown and reach for a robe.

She'd never needed one in Greece, she thought. The nights had been too hot except in the hotel, which had had air-conditioning. Each evening the chambermaid had arranged her flimsy confection of silk and lace in a fan shape on the bed, with a rose on the bodice and a hand-made chocolate on the pillow.

Later, in the taverna on Myros, she'd slept naked, kicking away even the thin sheet to the foot of the bed, her body grateful for the faint breeze sighing from the Aegean sea through the open window.

Moving quietly, she went downstairs to the kitchen and made herself a pot of coffee which she carried to the study.

She'd brought in the computer and set it up the night before, and if she couldn't sleep then she might as well start work. Begin to probe the real extent of the financial disaster facing her father.

Because it could be faced. She was convinced of that. James Fielding was a survivor. He would get over this heart attack, and the ensuing operation, and take up his life again. And somehow she had to salvage something from the wreckage—make sure there was something to give him hope.

She'd done some preliminary calculations of her own on the plane, partly to prevent herself thinking of other things, she realised, her mouth twisting, and had worked out how much she could afford to contribute. But the outlook was bleak. Even if she sold her London flat, and worked from this house, she'd struggle to pay the new mortgage.

Besides, she wasn't sure whether she could endure to live under this roof again for any length of time. There were too many bad memories.

Cressida had been a teenager, still mourning her mother, when she had learned of her father's decision to remarry. And her sense of shock, almost betrayal, had doubled when she'd discovered his choice of wife.

Looking back, she could see that she'd responded intolerantly to the newcomer, staring at her with resentful eyes.

Eloise had been a bit-part actress, her chief claim to fame as hostess on a second-rate TV quiz show. She was tall and full-breasted, her lips permanently set in a beguiling pout, her violet eyes wide, almost childlike.

Until she was crossed, Cressida thought wryly. And then they would narrow like a rattlesnake's.

As they'd done when she first met her new step-daughter. The hostility had not been one-sided by any means. Eloise had made it plain that she had little time for other women, and especially for a young girl just beginning to blossom out of gawkiness, although there was no way Cressy could ever have rivalled her volup-tuous charms.

Chalk and cheese, Cressy thought with sadness. And I was just a nuisance, someone to be sidelined, if not totally ignored.

And even when, urged by her father, she'd tried a few awkward overtures, she'd found herself completely rebuffed. Eventually she had acquired a reputation for being 'tricky', if not downright difficult. And James Fielding, unable to see he was being manipulated, had made his displeasure known to his daughter, creating a rift that had widened slowly but surely over the years.

Cressida had soon realised she was no longer wel-come in her own home. Even at Christmas Eloise had usually organised a ski-ing holiday for her husband and herself.

'Darling,' she'd said coaxingly when the first one was mooted. 'Cressida doesn't want to spend her vacations with a couple of old fogies. She has her own friends. Her own life.' Her steely gaze had fixed her stepdaugh-ter. 'Isn't that right?'

It had been easier to swallow her hurt and bewilder-ment and agree. She *had* had friends she could go to, and Uncle Robert and Aunt Barbara had always been there for her, their comfortable, untidy house a second home.

For a long time Cressida had convinced herself that the scales would eventually fall from her father's eyes and that he'd see Eloise's greed and self-absorption. But it had never happened. He'd been carried away by his passion for her—a passion that she had been careful to feed.

As for Eloise herself, Cressida was sure she'd looked at James Fielding and seen only a successful business-man, with a settled background and an attractive Georgian house not too far from London.

What she hadn't understood was that James's company had struggled to recover from the big recession of the eighties, or that James himself had faltered more than once as chairman, and was being encouraged to take early retirement.

Eloise had been too busy entertaining, enjoying weekend parties with amusing people, and being seen in all the right places.

Even after James's actual retirement she'd seen no need to scale down their style of living or their expenditure.

Alec Caravas had been a younger man with a fool-proof scheme for making them both instantly wealthy. Cressida could see how easily Eloise would have been seduced.

After all, she thought, I was planning to give up my job, my lifestyle, my independence. I shouldn't judge anyone else.

Her own meetings with her father over the past two years had been mainly confined to lunches in London, with the conversation constrained.

Perhaps I should have made more of an effort,

Cressida thought as she drank her coffee. Perhaps I should have played the hypocrite and pretended to like her. Even looked for her good points. Told myself that, whatever my personal feelings, she loved Dad and was making him happy.

Only, I never believed that. I just didn't want to be proved right quite so comprehensively.

She sighed, and turned resolutely to the computer screen. It was little use rehashing the past, she told herself forcibly. She had to try and salvage something from the present to ensure her father had a future.

She worked steadily for a couple of hours, but found little to comfort her.

Her father's company pension was indeed all that was left. All his other assets had been liquidised to make him a major shareholder in Paradise Grove. And he'd borrowed heavily too.

If he recovered from his heart attack, it would be to find himself insolvent, she realised unhappily.

His whole way of life would have to be downsized. She'd have to rent a larger flat, she thought, or even a house. Make a home for him—and Berry, who'd be needed more than ever. But how could she afford it?

I won't worry about that now, she told herself, glancing at her watch.

It was time she took a shower and dressed, and got over to the hospital again.

As she pushed back her chair, she noticed for the first time the small icon at the bottom of the screen indicating there was an e-mail message for her.

Someone else believes in an early start, Cressida thought wryly, as she clicked on to the little envelope and watched the message scroll down.

I am waiting for you.

The words were brief, almost laconic, but they had
the power to make her stiffen in shock and disbelief.

She twisted suddenly in her chair, staring over her
shoulder with frightened eyes.

The room was empty. And yet she felt Draco's presence as surely as if he was standing behind her, his hand
touching her shoulder.

She said, 'No,' and again, more fiercely, '*No*. It's not
true. It can't be…'

And heard the raw panic that shook her voice.

CHAPTER TWO

THERE was a rational explanation. There had to be.

Someone, somewhere, must be playing a trick on her, and had accidentally scored a bullseye.

All the way to the hospital Cressy kept telling herself feverishly that this was the way it had to be. That it must be one of her colleagues...

Except that they were all under the impression that she was still sunning herself on an island in the Aegean. She hadn't told anyone from work that she was back.

And, anyway, the message was too pointed—too personal to have come from anyone else but Draco. Wasn't it?

But how the hell did a Greek fisherman with one small, shabby boat and a half-built house manage to gain access to a computer, let alone have the technical know-how to send electronic mail halfway across Europe?

It made no sense.

Besides, he only knew my first name, she reminded herself with bewilderment. He can't possibly have traced me with that alone.

Her mind was still going round in ever decreasing circles as she went up in the lift to the Intensive Care Unit. But she steadied herself when the sister in charge met her with the good news that her father's condition had greatly improved.

'He's asleep at the moment, but you may sit with him.' Calm eyes looked squarely into Cressida's. 'You can be relied on not to make emotional scenes, Miss Fielding? He really doesn't need that kind of disturbance.'

'Of course not.' Cressy said steadily. 'I just want him to get better.'

She fetched some coffee from the machine in the corridor, then quietly took up her vigil, forcing herself to composure. She couldn't afford to send out any negative vibrations.

And she hadn't time to worry about mysterious e-mail messages or who might have generated them. Her father was her priority now, and nothing else could be allowed to matter.

That worrying grey tinge seemed to have gone from James Fielding's face. He looked more his old self again, she thought, surreptitiously crossing her fingers.

If he continued to make good progress he could soon be moved to a private room, she told herself. The premiums on his private health insurance had been allowed to lapse, but she would pay.

She said under her breath. 'I'll look after you, Daddy—whatever it takes. I'll make sure you're all right.'

He woke up once, gave her a faint smile, and fell asleep again. But it was enough.

Apart from the hum of the various machines, the unit was quite peaceful. And very hot, Cressy thought, undoing another button on her cream cotton shirt.

Almost as hot as it had been in Greece.

For a moment she could feel the beat of the sun on her head, see its dazzle on the water and hear the slap of the small waves against the bow of the caique as it took her to Myros.

*   *   *

Myros…

She noticed it the day she arrived, when she walked across the cool marble floor of her hotel bedroom, out on to the balcony, and looked across the sparkle of the sea at the indigo smudge on the horizon.

As she tipped the porter who'd brought up her luggage, she asked, 'What is that island?'

'That, *thespinis*, is Myros.'

'*Myros.*' She repeated the name softly under her breath.

She stayed where she was, fingers lightly splayed on the balustrade, lifting her face to the sun, listening to the distant wash of the sea and the rasp of the cicadas in the vast gardens below.

She could feel the worries and tensions of the past months sliding away from her.

She thought, with bewilderment and growing content, I really need this holiday. I didn't realize it, but Martin was quite right.

Her work was always meticulous, but she'd made a couple of mistakes in the last few weeks. Nothing too dire, and nothing that couldn't be swiftly put right without inconvenience to the client, but disturbing just the same.

Martin had looked at her over his glasses. 'When was the last time you took a break, Cress? And I don't mean Christmas and the usual Bank Holidays. I mean a real, live, away-from-it-all, lie-in-the-sun break. The sort that ordinary people have.'

'I have time off,' she had said. 'Last time I decorated my sitting room at the flat.'

'Exactly.' He'd sat back in his chair, his gaze inflexible. 'So you take the rest of the afternoon off, you visit a travel agent and you book yourself at least three weeks of total relaxation in some bit of the Mediterranean. Then get yourself some sun cream and a selection of pulp fiction and go. And that's an order,' he had added as Cressy had begun to protest pressure of work.

She'd obeyed mutinously, agreeing to the travel company's first suggestion of an all-inclusive trip to the latest in the Hellenic Imperial hotel chain.

'They're all the last word in luxury,' the travel clerk had enthused. 'And there's a full programme of sport and entertainment on offer. This one only opened recently, which is why there are still a few rooms available.'

'Anything,' Cressy had said, and had put down her gold card.

She might have arrived under protest, but she couldn't pretend she wasn't impressed.

For the first few days she simply relaxed under an umbrella on one of the sun terraces, swam in each of the three pools, had a couple of tennis lessons, and tried her hand, gingerly, at windsurfing. She also sampled all of the restaurants on the complex.

For once the brochure had spoken nothing but the truth, she thought wryly. The Hellenic Imperial was the height of opulence. The service was excellent, and no element of comfort had been overlooked.

But by the end of the first week Cressy was beginning to feel that it was all too perfect.

Most of the other guests seemed perfectly content to stay on the complex and be waited on hand and foot, but Cressy was restless. She rented a car, and took in the sights. The island's capital, with its harbour full of glamorous yachts and its sophisticated shopping facilities, left her cold. She much preferred driving up throat-tightening mountain roads to see a church with famous frescoes, sampling dark, spicy wine in a local vineyard, or drinking tiny cups of thick, sweet coffee in *kafeneions* in remote villages.

But, more and more, she found herself looking across the glittering sapphire of the Aegean and wondering exactly what lay there on the horizon.

One morning, when she was changing some money at Reception, she said casually, 'How do I get to Myros?'

The clerk could not have looked more astonished if she'd asked what time the next space ship left for the moon.

'Myros, *thespinis*?' he repeated carefully.

Cressy nodded. 'It's not that far away. I presume there's a ferry.'

He pursed his lips. 'There are boats,' he said discouragingly. 'But tourists do not go there, Kyria Fielding.'

'Why not?'

He shrugged. 'Because everything they want is here,' he returned with unshakeable logic.

'Nevertheless,' Cressy said equably, biting back a smile, 'I'd like to know where the boats leave from.'

The clerk looked almost distressed. 'You don't like this hotel, *thespinis*? You find it lacking in some way?'

'Not at all,' she assured him. 'I'd just like a change.'

'But there is nothing on Myros, *kyria*. It has no hotels, no facilities. It is a place for farmers and fishermen.'

'It sounds perfect,' Cressy said, and left him in midprotest.

She was aware of curious glances as she sat in the bow of the caique watching Myros turn from an indistinct blur into a tall, mountainous ridge, the lower slopes softened by patches of greenery. She was without question the only foreigner on the boat, and the skipper, who looked like an amiable pirate, had initially demurred over accepting her fare.

As the caique traversed the shoreline, Cressy saw long stretches of pale sand, sheltered by jagged rocks.

The fishermen and the farmers have been lucky so far, she thought. Because this place looks ripe for exploitation to me.

The harbour was only tiny, with no smart boats among the battered caiques. Row upon row of small white houses seemed to be tumbling headlong towards the narrow waterfront where fishing nets were spread to dry.

Somewhere a church bell was ringing, its sound cool and sonorous in the hot, shimmering air.

Cressy found her heart clenching in sudden excitement and pleasure.

Her canvas beach bag slung over her shoulder, she scrambled ashore.

There was a sprinkling of tavernas and coffee shops on the harbourside, most of them frequented by elderly men playing a very fast and intense form of backgammon.

Cressy chose a table under an awning at the largest, waiting while the proprietor, a stocky man in jeans and a white shirt, finished hosing down the flagstones.

'Thespinis?' His smile was cordial enough, but the black eyes were shrewdly assessing.

Cressy asked for an iced Coke, and, when he brought it, enquired if there was anywhere she could hire a car.

The smile broadened regretfully. The only vehicles on Myros, she was told, were Jeeps and pick-up trucks,

and none were for rent. The roads, the *kyria* must understand, were not good.

Well, I knew they didn't cater for tourists, Cressy
reminded herself philosophically. But it was a setback.

She said, 'I saw beaches, *kyrie*. Can I reach them on
foot?'

He nodded. 'It is possible, *thespinis*. Our finest beach
is only a kilometre from here.' He paused thoughtfully,
fingering his heavy black moustache. 'But there is a
better way.' From a storeroom at the back of the taverna, he produced an ancient bicycle. 'It belonged to
my sister,' he explained. 'But she is in Athens.'

'And you'll lend it to me?' Cressy raised her eyebrows. 'That's very kind.'

He shrugged. 'She will be happy for you to use it. It
is an honour for her.'

'But how do you know I'll bring it back?'

The smile became almost indulgent. 'When the *kyria*
wishes to leave Myros, she must return here. Also, she
must eat, and my taverna has good fish. The best.' He
nodded. 'You will come back, *thespinis*.'

Cressy hadn't ridden a bicycle for years. She waited
while the proprietor, whose name was Yannis, cere-
moniously dusted the saddle for her, then mounted awkwardly.

She said, 'I hope it lasts the distance, *kyrie*.'

'A kilometre is not too far.' He paused. 'I do not
recommend that you go further than that, thespinis.'

'We'll see,' Cressy said cheerfully. 'Once I get the
hang of it, I may do the grand tour.'

Yannis's face was suddenly serious. 'Go to the beach
only, *thespinis*. I advise it. Beyond it the road is bad.
Very bad.'

Now, why did she get the feeling that Yannis was

warning her about more than the state of the road? Cressy wondered, as she wobbled away.

But he hadn't been exaggerating. Outside the small town, the road soon deteriorated into a dirt track, with olive groves on one side and the sea on the other, and Cressy had to concentrate hard on keeping her eccentric machine upright, and avoiding the largest stones and deepest potholes.

Apart from the whisper of the sea, and the faint breeze rustling the silver leaves of the olive trees, Cressy felt as if she was enclosed in a silent, shimmering landscape. She was glad of the broad straw hat protecting her blonde hair.

The beach was soon reached, but, she saw with disappointment, it was only a narrow strip of sand with a lot of pebbles and little shade.

The others I saw were much better, she thought. Yannis can't have meant this one.

In spite of the road, she was beginning, against all odds, to enjoy her unexpected cycle ride, and decided to press on to one of the secluded coves she'd glimpsed from the ferry.

Ten minutes later, she was beginning to regret her decision. The gradient on her route had taken a sharp upward turn, and her elderly bone-shaker was no mountain bike.

This must have been what Yannis meant, she thought grimly. Certainly it warranted a warning.

She halted, to have a drink from the bottle of water which he'd pressed on her and consider what to do next.

Myros was only a small island, she argued inwardly, and the next beach couldn't be too far away. So, it might be better to leave the bike at the side of the track—after all, no one in his right mind would steal it—and proceed on foot.

She laid the ancient machine tenderly on its side in the shade of an olive tree, blew it a kiss, and walked on.

She'd gone about five hundred yards when she first heard the music, only faint, but unmistakably Greek, with its strong underlying rhythm. Cressy paused, breathless from her continued climb, and listened, her brows drawing together.

She swore softly under her breath. 'I don't believe it,' she muttered. 'I've come all this way in this heat, only to find someone else's beach party.'

She was going to walk on, but then sudden curiosity got the better of her, and, letting the music guide her, she moved quietly through the scrub and stones to the edge of the cliff. There was a track of sorts leading down to the pale crescent of sand below, but Cressy ignored that, moving to slightly higher ground where she could get an overall view of the beach.

The first thing she saw was a small caique, with faded blue paint and its sails furled, moored just offshore. But that appeared to be deserted.

Then she looked down, and the breath caught in her throat.

Below her, alone on the sand, a man was dancing.

Arms flung wide, head back, his face lifted to the sun, he swayed, and dipped to the ground, and leapt, his entire body given over to the sheer joy of living— and the raw power of the music.

And totally absorbed in his response to it, thought Cressy. Clearly nothing else existed for him at this moment.

She dropped to her knees in the shelter of a dried and

spindly shrub and watched, amused at first, but gradually becoming more entranced.

She'd seen demonstrations of *syrtaki* at the hotel, of course, but never performed with this wild, elemental force.

This man seemed completely at home in his solitary environment, Cressy told herself in bewilderment, as if he was somehow part of the sea, and the rocks, and the harsh brilliant sunlight, and shared their common spirit. Or the reincarnation of some pagan god...

She halted right there.

Now she was just being fanciful, she thought with self-derision.

He might be a wonderful dancer, but what she was actually seeing was a waiter from one of the hotels on the other island, practising his after-dinner routine for the tourists.

But not from my hotel, she thought. Or I'd have remembered...

Because he wasn't just a beautiful dancer. He was beautiful in other ways, too.

He was taller than average, and magnificently built, with broad, muscular shoulders, narrow hips and endless legs, his only covering a pair of ragged denim shorts which left little to the imagination.

The thick, dark hair, curling down on to the nape of his neck, gleamed like silk in the sunshine, and his skin was like burnished bronze.

To her shock, Cressy found her mouth was suddenly dry, her pulses drumming in unaccustomed and unwelcome excitement. She realised, too, there was an odd, trembling ache deep within her.

What the hell am I doing? she asked frantically, as she lifted herself cautiously to her feet and backed away. I'm an intelligent woman. I go for brains, not brawn. Or I would if I was interested in any kind of involvement, she reminded herself hastily.

Besides, this brand of obvious physicality leaves me cold. I'm not in the market for—holiday bait.

She was being unfair, and she knew it as she walked on, her pace quickening perceptibly.

After all, the lone dancer could have no idea he had an audience. He'd created his own private world of passion and movement, and if its intrinsic sensuality had sent her into meltdown then that was her problem, not his.

All the same, she was glad when the music faded from earshot. Although the image in her mind might not be so easy to dismiss, she realised ruefully.

'I don't know what's happening to me, but I don't like it,' she said under her breath, lengthening her stride.

A further five minutes' walk brought her to another cove, and this one was deserted, she noted as she scrambled thankfully down to the sand.

She stood for a moment, listening to the silence, then spread her towel in the shade of a rock, kicked off her canvas shoes, and slipped out of her navy cotton trousers and shirt to reveal the simple matching bikini beneath.

The sea was like cooling balm against her overheated skin. She waded out until the water was waist-high, then slid gently forward into its embrace, breaking into her strong, easy crawl.

When she eventually got tired, she turned on her back and floated, her eyes closed against the dazzle of the sun.

She felt completely at peace. London, the office and its problems seemed a lifetime away. Even the rift with her father no longer seemed quite so hurtful—or so insoluble. Eloise had driven a wedge between them, but—with care—wedges could be removed. Maybe she'd needed to distance herself in order to see that.

Back under her rock, she towelled herself down, applied sun cream with a lavish hand, drank some more water, then lay down on her front. She reached behind her and undid the clip of her bikini top. A suntan might not be fashionable, but it was inevitable that she would gain a little colour in this heat, and she didn't want any unsightly marks to spoil the effect in the low-backed dresses she'd brought.

She felt bonelessly relaxed, even a little drowsy, as she pillowed her cheek on her folded arms.

There's nothing I can't handle, she told herself with satisfaction as she drifted off to sleep.

She would never be certain what woke her. There was just an odd feeling of disquiet—a sudden chill, as if a cloud had covered the sun—that permeated her pleasant dream and broke its spell.

Cressy forced open her unwilling eyelids. For a moment she could see nothing, because the dazzle of the sun was too strong.

Then, slowly, she realised that she was no longer alone.

That there was someone lying on the sand beside her, only a few feet away. Someone tall and bronzed in denim shorts, who was—dear God—smiling at her.

She wanted to scream, but her throat muscles seemed suddenly paralysed. And she couldn't move either because she'd undone her top.

When she found her voice, it sounded small and husky. 'What do you want?'

His smile widened. His mouth, she saw, was firm, although his lower lip had a betrayingly sensuous curve, and his teeth were very white. For the rest of him, he had a straight nose, just fractionally too long for classical beauty, strongly accented cheekbones, and deepset eyes the colour of agate flecked with gold.

He also needed a shave.

He said, 'Why did you not come down and dance with me?' His voice was deep, with a distinct undercurrent of amusement, and he spoke in English.

It was the last thing she'd expected him to say, and for a moment she was stunned. Then she rallied.

'I don't know what you mean.'

'Ah, no.' He shook his head reprovingly. 'You should not tell lies—especially when you are so bad at it. Your eyes will always give you away.'

'That's ridiculous,' Cressy said with hostility. 'And also impertinent. You know nothing about me.'

'I know that you were watching me from the cliff, and then you ran away.' The return was imperturbable.

'I didn't run,' Cressy said with as much dignity as she could evoke when she was lying, prone, wearing only the bottom half of a bikini. 'I just wanted to find some peace and quiet. And I didn't mean to disturb you. Please go back to your—rehearsal.'

'That is finished for the day. Now it is time to eat.' He reached behind him and produced a small rucksack.

Cressy groaned inwardly. How on earth was she going to get rid of him, she wondered wildly, without insulting his Greek machismo? She was uneasily aware of how isolated this little beach was. And that they were both almost naked. The last thing she needed to do was provoke him in any way. Even to anger.

She made a business of looking at her watch. 'So, it

is. Well, I must get back to the village. Yannis is expecting me to eat at his taverna.'

'But not in the middle of the day,' he said. 'In the middle of the day he likes to drink coffee and play *tavli*. He'll cook for you tonight.'

'I don't think so.' Cressy made a discreet effort to fasten the hook on her bikini top. 'I have to get the evening ferry back to Alakos.'

Her unwanted neighbour watched her struggles with interest, but didn't volunteer his assistance as she'd been half afraid he might. 'You are staying in a hotel on Alakos?'

'Yes.' At the third attempt, Cressy managed the hook, and felt marginally more secure. 'At the Hellenic Imperial.'

'The Imperial? *Po po po.*' His dark brows lifted. 'You would need to be very rich to stay at such a place.'

'Not at all,' Cressy said with a certain crispness, wondering if he was planning to kidnap her and hold her to ransom. 'I work for my living like everyone else.'

'Ah—you are a model, perhaps—or an actress?' He produced a paper bag from his rucksack and opened it. Cressy saw that it contained pitta bread with some kind of filling.

'Of course not,' she denied swiftly. 'I work in an office—as a taxation accountant.' She reached for her shirt. 'And now I must be going.'

'It is a long time until evening—and your ferry.' He divided the envelope of pitta bread into two and held out half to her, using the paper bag as a plate.

'No,' Cressy said. 'It's very kind of you, but I couldn't—possibly.'

He leaned across and put the improvised plate on the corner of her towel.

'Why are you frightened?' He sounded as if he was merely expressing a friendly interest.

'I'm not.'

He sighed. 'You are lying again, *matia mou*. Now eat, and tell me about your work in England, and later we will swim. And do not tell me you cannot swim,' he added, as her lips parted in negation, 'because I too was watching.'

Cressy sat very upright. She said, quietly and coldly. 'Does it occur to you, *kyrie*, that I might not want to spend the afternoon with you? That I prefer to be alone?'

'Yes,' he said. 'But that will change when you know me better. And no one so young and so lovely should wish to be alone. It is a sad thing.'

There was lamb tucked into the pitta bread. The scent of it was making her mouth water.

She glared at him. 'I've no taste for meaningless compliments, *kyrie*.'

He said, 'Nor do I, *thespinis*. You know that you are young, so accept that you are also beautiful. And my name is Draco.' He smiled at her. 'Now eat your food, and don't be afraid any more.'

But that, thought Cressy, looking down at the pattern on the towel—or anywhere rather than at him—that was easier said than done.

CHAPTER THREE

IN SPITE of all Cressy's misgivings about the risks of her situation—and they were many and various—she supposed she had better accept Draco's offer of food. One placatory gesture, she told herself, and then she would go.

If she was allowed to, said a small, unpleasant voice in her head. She'd seen his athleticism when he was dancing. She might be able to out-think him, but did she really imagine she could outrun him up that lethal track?

So much for striking out and being independent, she derided herself. She should have stayed safely in the hotel precincts.

She had expected she would have to force a few mouthfuls past the unremitting tightness of her throat, but to her astonishment the lamb, which had been roasted with herbs and was served with a light lemon dressing and sliced black olives, tasted absolutely wonderful, and she finished every bite.

'It was good?' Draco asked as Cressy wiped her lips and fingers on a tissue.

'It was terrific,' she admitted. She gave him a taut smile. 'You speak English very well.'

His own smile was slow, touched with overt reminiscence. 'I had good teachers.'

'Women, no doubt,' Cressy heard herself saying tartly, and could have bitten her tongue in half. The last thing she needed to do was antagonise him, and his personal life was none of her business anyway, so what had possessed her to make such a comment?

She saw his face harden, the firm mouth suddenly compressed. For a moment she felt the crackle of tension in the air between them like live electricity, then, totally unexpectedly, he began to laugh.

'You are astute, *thespinis*.' Propped on one elbow, he gave her a long and leisurely assessment, missing nothing, making her feel naked under his agate gaze. 'But my grammar—my pronunciation—are not perfect. I am sure there is room for improvement—with the right help.'

Cressy was burning from head to foot, and it had nothing to do with the sun.

She said, 'I'm afraid that you'll have to find another tutor, *kyrie*. I'm not in the market.'

'Life has taught me that most things are for sale, *kyria*—if the price is right.'

There was real danger here. Every instinct she possessed was screaming it at her.

She said coolly and clearly, 'But I am not. And now I think I'd better go.'

'As you wish.' The powerful shoulders lifted in a negligent shrug. 'But understand this. I take only what is freely given. Nothing more. And, in any case, you are the stranger within my gates, and you have eaten my bread, so you have nothing to fear.'

He lifted himself lithely to his feet. 'Now I am going to swim. Naturally, I hope you will still be here when I return, but the choice is yours, *kyria*.'

For a moment he stood looking down at her. He said softly, 'So beautiful, and such a sharp tongue. And yet so afraid of life. What a pity.'

The damned nerve of him, Cressy seethed, watching

him lope down the sand. Translating her natural caution into cowardice.

And, for all his assurances, it was quite obvious that he was just another good-looking Greek on the make. She'd seen it happening at the hotel. Watched them targeting the single women, the divorcees, the ones with hunger in their eyes.

Cressy had avoided their attentions by being busy and absorbed.

But I should have known I couldn't escape for ever, she thought angrily.

Except that she could. Draco was swimming strongly away from the beach. She could see the darkness of his head against the glitter of the sea.

All she had to do was grab her things, put on her shoes, and she would be free.

Free to go back to the village and wait for the evening ferry, at any rate, she reminded herself with an inward groan. Where Draco would know exactly where to find her...

She was caught in a trap of her own making, it seemed. And to sneak away as if she was genuinely scared appeared oddly demeaning anyway.

It would certainly be more dignified to stay where she was. To treat any overtures he might make with cool and dismissive courtesy. And then return to the village in time for a meal at the taverna and her homeward boat trip exactly as she'd planned.

Maybe Draco needed to learn that, for all his good looks and sexual charisma, not all tourists were pushovers.

And he'd virtually guaranteed that she was safe with him, that traditional Greek hospitality would remain paramount, and, in a strange way, she believed him.

Unless, of course, she chose differently. And there was no chance of that.

So she would stay—for a while. Because she was in control of the situation.

But only because he's allowing you to be, niggled the small, irritating voice.

Ignoring it, Cressy reapplied her sun cream, put on her dark glasses and reached for the book she'd brought with her.

When Draco came back he'd find her composed and occupied, and not prepared to be involved in any more verbal tangles.

Distance was the thing, she told herself. And this beach was quite big enough for both of them.

She did not hear his return up the beach—he moved with the noiseless, feline grace of a panther—but she sensed that he was there, just the same. She kept her shoulder slightly turned and her eyes fixed rigidly on the printed page, a silent indication that the story was too gripping to brook interruption.

At the same time she'd expected her signals to be ignored. That he'd at least make some comment about her decision to remain. But as the soundless minutes passed Cressy realised she might be mistaken.

She ventured a swift sideways look, and saw with unreasoning annoyance that Draco was lying face down on his towel, his eyes closed, apparently fast asleep.

She bit her lip, and turned her page with a snap.

But it was all to no avail, she realised five minutes later. She simply couldn't concentrate. She was far too conscious of the man stretched out beside her.

She closed her book and studied him instead. She wondered how old he was. At least thirty, she surmised. Probably slightly more. He wore no jewellery—no me-

dallions, earrings or other gifts from grateful ladies. Just
an inexpensive wristwatch, she noted. And no wedding
ring either, although that probably meant nothing. If
part of his livelihood involved charming foreign woman
holidaymakers, he would hardly want to advertise the
fact that he was married.

And she could just imagine his poor wife, she thought
with asperity, staring up at the sky. Dressed in the ubiq-
uitous black, cooking, cleaning and working in the
fields and olive groves while her husband pursued his
other interests on the beaches and beside the swimming
pools on Alakos—and nice work if you could get it.

'So what have you decided about me?'

Cressy, starting violently, turned her head and found
Draco watching her, his mouth twisted in amusement
and all signs of slumber fled.

There was no point in pretending or prevaricating.
She said flatly, 'I don't have enough evidence to make
a judgement.'

His brows lifted. 'What can I tell you?'

'Nothing.' Cressy shrugged. 'After all, it's unlikely
that we'll meet again. Let's be content to remain strangers.'

'That is truly what you want?' His tone was curious.

'I've just said so.'

'Then why did you stare at me as if you were trying
to see into my heart?'

'Is that what I was doing?' Cressy made a business
of applying more sun cream to her legs. 'I—I didn't
realise.'

He shook his head reprovingly. 'Another foolish lie,
matia mou.'

Cressy replaced the cap on the sun cream as if she
was wringing someone's neck.

'Very well,' she said. 'If you want to play silly games. What do you do for a living, *kyrie*?'

He lifted a shoulder. 'A little of this. A little of that.'

I can imagine. Aloud, she said, 'That's hardly an answer. I suppose the caique moored in the next cove is yours, and I've seen you dance, so I'd guess you're primarily a fisherman but you also do hotel work entertaining the guests. Am I right?'

'I said you were astute, *thespinis*,' he murmured. 'You read me as you would a balance sheet.'

'It really wasn't that difficult.'

'Truly?' There was slight mockery in his tone. 'Now, shall I tell you about you, I wonder?'

'There's very little to say,' Cressy said swiftly. 'You already know what my work is.'

'Ah.' The dark eyes held hers steadily for a moment. 'But I was not thinking of work.' He got to his feet, dusting sand from his legs. 'However, you have reminded me, *thespinis*, that I cannot enjoy the sun and your company any longer. I have to prepare for this evening's performance.' He slung his towel over his shoulder and picked up his rucksack.

He smiled down at her. '*Kalispera, matia mou.*'

'You keep calling me that, *kyrie*,' Cressy said with a snap, angrily aware of an odd disappointment at his departure. 'What does it mean?'

For one fleeting moment his hand brushed her cheek, pushing back an errant strand of silky hair.

He said softly, 'It means "my eyes". And my name, if you recall, is Draco. Until we meet again.'

He'd hardly touched her, Cressy repeated to herself for the fourth or fifth time. There was nothing to get upset about. He'd pushed her hair behind her ear, and that was all. He hadn't touched her breast or any of her exposed skin, as he could so easily have done.

All that time she'd carefully kept her distance. Built the usual invisible wall around herself.

And then, with one brief, casual gesture, he'd invaded her most personal space. And there hadn't been a damned thing she could do about it.

Oh, there'd been nothing overtly sexual in his touch—she couldn't accuse him of that—yet she'd felt the tingle of her body's response in the innermost core of her being. Known a strange, draining languor as he had walked away. And a sharp, almost primitive need to call him back again.

And that was what she couldn't accept—couldn't come to terms with. That sudden dangerous weakness. The unexpected vulnerability.

God knows what I'd have done if he'd really come on to me, she brooded unhappily.

But the most galling aspect of all was that he'd been the one who'd chosen to leave, and not herself.

I should have gone the moment I woke up and saw him there, Cressy told herself in bitter recrimination. I should have been very English and very outraged at having my privacy disturbed. End of story.

For that matter, the story was over now, she admitted with an inward shrug. She just hadn't been the one to write *Finis*, that was all. And, while she might regret it, there was no need to eat her heart out either.

When she'd heard the thrum of the caique's engine as it passed the cove she'd tried hard to keep her attention fixed on her book. When she'd finally risked a quick glance she had found, to her fury, that he was waving to her from the tiller.

But at least he had been sailing in the opposite direction to the harbour, and she wouldn't run the risk of bumping into him there while she was waiting for the ferry.

And now she had the cove to herself again, just as she'd wanted. Except that it was no longer the peaceful sanctuary that she'd discovered a few hours before. Because she felt restless, suddenly, and strangely dissatisfied.

She wanted to cry out, It's all spoiled, like an angry, thwarted child.

But there was nothing to be gained by sitting about counting her wrongs, she thought with a saving grace of humour.

She went for a last swim, relishing the freshness of the water now a slight breeze had risen, hoping wryly that it would cool her imagination as well as her body.

She collected the bicycle and stood for a moment, debating what to do next. It was too early for dinner and, now that the searing afternoon heat had abated, she decided she might as well see what remained of Myros. It was only a small island, and the circular tour would probably take no more than an hour.

It was very much a working island, she soon realised. The interior might be rocky and inhospitable, but on the lower slopes fields had been ploughed and vines and olives were being cultivated, along with orchards of citrus fruits. The scattered hamlets she passed through seemed prosperous enough, and the few people she encountered offered friendly smiles and greetings.

And, contrary to what Yannis had suggested, the road to the north of the island even had some sort of surface.

So Cressy was disconcerted to find her path suddenly blocked by tall wrought-iron gates and a stone wall.

It seemed that the public road had suddenly become private.

Cressy dismounted and tried the gates, but they were securely locked and she could only rattle them in mild frustration. Beyond them she could see a drive winding upwards between olive groves, then, intriguingly, curving away out of sight, making it impossible to guess what lay further on.

She walked along the side of the wall for a while, but it seemed to stretch for ever, and eventually she was forced to retrace her steps.

Apparently, a whole section of the island had been turned into a no-go area. And all she could do was turn back.

After that disappointment, the puncture was almost inevitable.

Cressy brought her untrustworthy steed to a juddering halt and surveyed the damage, cursing herself mentally for having been lured into such an extensive trip.

Now she was faced with a long walk back to the port, pushing the bicycle.

The breeze had strengthened, whipping up the dust from the road and sending irritating particles into her eyes and mouth. She'd finished her water some time before, and she felt hot, thirsty and out of sorts. What was more, she suspected she was getting a blister on her foot.

From now on, she promised herself, she'd confine her activities to the grounds of the Hellenic Imperial.

She'd limped on for another quarter of a mile when she heard the sound of a vehicle on the road behind her.

'More dust,' she muttered, dragging herself and the bicycle on to the stony verge.

A battered pick-up truck roared past, but not before Cressy had managed to catch a glimpse of the driver.

She said a despairing, 'Oh, no—it can't be...' as the truck braked sharply and began to reverse back to where she was standing.

He said, 'How good to meet again so soon. I did not expect it.'

She said crisply, 'Nor I. You were on board a boat, *kyrie*. Now you're driving a truck. What next, I wonder?'

'Probably my own two feet, *thespinis*—like you.' Draco slanted a smile at her through the open window. 'Get in, and I will drive you back to the port.'

'I'm enjoying the walk,' Cressy said regally, and he sighed.

'More lies, *matia mou*. When will you learn?' He swung himself down from the truck, picked up the bicycle and tossed it onto a pile of sacks in the back of the vehicle, then gave Cressy a measuring look. 'You wish to travel like that, or with me?'

Glaring at him, Cressy scrambled into the passenger seat. 'Do you always get your own way?'

He shrugged. 'Why not?'

She could think of a hundred reasons without repeating herself, but she said nothing, sitting beside him in mutinous silence as the pick-up lurched down the track.

At least he'd changed out of those appalling shorts, she thought, stealing a lightning glance from under her lashes. He was now wearing clean but faded jeans and a white shirt, open at the neck with the sleeves turned back over his tanned forearms. And he seemed to have shaved.

All ready for the evening conquests, no doubt.

After a while, he said, 'You are not in a very good mood after your day on the beach.'

Cressy shrugged. 'It started well,' she said stonily. 'Then went downhill fast.'

'As you tried to do on Yannis's bicycle?' He was grinning. 'Not wise.'

'So I discovered,' she admitted tautly. 'Now all I want is to get back to Alakos.'

'You don't like my island?'

'It isn't that at all,' she denied swiftly. 'But I'm hot, dusty, and my hair's full of salt. I need a shower, a cold drink and a meal.'

'*Katavaleno*. I understand.' He swerved to avoid a major pothole. 'So, tell me what you think of Myros?'

'I like what I've seen.' Cressy paused. 'But some of it seems to be cordoned off.'

'Ah,' he said. 'You have been to the north of the island. Some rich people have their houses there.'

'They clearly like their privacy.' She frowned. 'Don't the islanders mind?'

'There is enough room for all of us.' He shrugged. 'If they wish to stay behind high walls, that is their problem.'

There was a silence, then he said, 'When I saw you, you were limping. Why?'

Cressy fought back a gasp.

She said curtly, 'You don't miss much, do you? My foot's a little sore, that's all.'

'You have sprained your ankle?'

'No—nothing like that.'

'What, then?'

Cressy hesitated. 'It's just a small blister.' She forced a smile. 'I seem to have lost the knack of walking.'

He nodded. 'And also of living, I think.'

Cressy flushed. 'So you keep saying. But it's not true. I have a terrific life. I'm very successful, and very happy. And you have no right to imply otherwise,' she added hotly. 'You don't know me, or anything about me.'

'I am trying,' he said. 'But you don't make it easy.'

'Then perhaps you should take the hint,' she flashed. 'Find a more willing subject to analyse.'

She was suddenly thrown across the seat as Draco swung the wheel, turning his ramshackle vehicle on to the verge, where he stopped.

'What are you doing?' Cressy struggled to regain her balance, feeling her breath quicken as Draco turned slowly to face her.

'You think you are unwilling?' The agate eyes glittered at her. 'But you are wrong. You are only unaware.'

He allowed that to sink in, nodding slightly at her indrawn breath, then went on, 'As for the happiness and the success you speak of, I see no such things in you. A woman who is fulfilled has an inner light. Her eyes shine, her skin blooms. But when I look into your eyes I see sadness and fear, *matia mou*.'

He paused. 'And not all high walls are made of stone. Remember that.'

Cressy's back was rigid. She said raggedly, 'I'm sure this chat-up line works with some people, but not with me, *kyrie*. You're insolent, and arrogant, and I'd prefer to walk the rest of the way.'

Draco restarted the truck. 'You will hurt no one but yourself, *thespinis*. And you will walk nowhere until that blister has received attention,' he added curtly. 'So don't be a fool.'

She had never been so angry. She sat with her arms

wrapped round her body, damming back the words of
fury and condemnation that threatened to choke her.
Fighting back tears, too, unexpected and inexplicable.

She didn't move until the truck stopped outside
Yannis's taverna, and she turned to make a measured
and final exit, only to find herself fighting with the re-
calcitrant door catch.

Draco had no such problems, she realised with gritted
teeth as he jumped out of the driving seat and appeared
beside her. In a second the door was open, and Cressy
found herself being lifted out of the passenger side and
carried round the side of the taverna to a flight of white-
painted stone steps.

Gasping, she began to struggle, trying vainly to get
her arms free so that she could hit him. 'How dare you?
You bastard. Put me down—put me down now.'

She saw Yannis in a doorway with a plump, pretty
woman in a faded red dress standing beside him, their
faces masks of astonishment. Heard Draco bark some
kind of command in his own language as he started up
the steps with Cressy still pinned helplessly against his
chest.

The door at the top of the stairs was standing open,
and Cressy was carried through it into a corridor lined
by half a dozen doors in dark, carved wood.

Draco opened the nearest and shouldered his way in.
It was a large room, its pale walls tinged with the glow
of sunset from the half-open shutters at the window.

The floor was tiled and there was a chest of drawers,
a clothes cupboard and a large bed covered in immaculate white linen, towards which she was being relentlessly carried.

And her anger gave way to swift, nerve-shredding
panic.

As Draco put her down on the coverlet, she heard herself whisper, 'No—please…' and hated the note of pleading in her voice.

Draco straightened, his face cold, his mouth a thin line. 'Do not insult me. I have told Maria to come to you. Now, wait there.'

As he reached the door, he was met by the plump woman carrying towels, a basket containing soap and shampoo, and, most welcome of all, a bottle of drinking water.

She rounded on Draco, her voice shrill and scolding, and he grinned down at her, lifting his hands in mock surrender as he went out, closing the door behind him.

Maria looked at Cressy, her dark eyes unwelcoming. She said in slow, strongly accented English, 'Who are you, *kyria*, and what are you doing here?'

Cressy said wearily, 'I don't think I know any more.' And at last her precarious self-control slipped, and she burst into a flood of tears.

CHAPTER FOUR

SHE hadn't intended it, but it was probably the best thing she could have done. Because next moment she'd been swept into Maria's embrace and was being cooed at in Greek, while a surprisingly gentle hand stroked her hair.

When the choking sobs began to subside, she was urged into the little tiled shower-room.

'All will be well, little one,' Maria said as she left her alone. 'You will see. Men,' she added in a tone of robust disapproval.

The warm water and shampoo provided a healing therapy of their own, and Cressy felt almost human again as she wandered back into the bedroom with the largest towel wrapped round her like a sarong.

She checked in surprise because her discarded clothing seemed to have vanished. True, she hadn't been looking forward to putting it on again, but, apart from a change of underwear in her bag, it was all she had. And she could hardly travel back to Alakos in a towel.

Then she saw that there was something lying on the bed—a dress in filmy white cotton, with a full skirt and a square neck embroidered with flowers.

She heard a sound at the door, and turned eagerly. 'Oh, Maria,' she began, and stopped, her breath catching in her throat, as Draco strode into the room.

She swallowed, her hand instinctively going to the knot that secured the towel in place.

She said icily, 'Get out of here—now. Or I'll scream for Maria.'

'You will need strong lungs. Maria is busy in the kitchen.' He put down the bowl he was carrying on the table beside the bed. 'And I am here on an errand of mercy. Let me see your foot.'

'My foot is fine.'

'You wish to have an infection?' His tone was inflexible. 'And spend the rest of your vacation in hospital?' He pointed to the bed. 'Sit down.'

'You have an answer for everything,' Cressy said as she mutinously obeyed. 'I suppose you trained as a doctor between fishing and dancing in restaurants.'

His mouth twisted. 'No, *thespinis*. I took a course in common sense.'

He knelt in front of her and lifted her foot gently to examine it. His fingers were gentle and cool, and she felt a strange shiver of awareness glide between her shoulder blades and down her spine. He glanced up.

'I am hurting you?'

'No.' Cressy bit her lip, trying to appear composed. But it wasn't easy. The clean, male scent of him seemed to fill her consciousness, and she found herself breathing more deeply, inhaling the faint fragrance of soap and clean linen. The silky black curls were inches from her hand, and she wondered how they would feel as her fingers caressed them.

Beneath the towel, she could feel her skin warming in swift, unbidden excitement. Feel her hardening nipples graze against the rough fabric...

Oh, God, what am I doing?

Aloud, she said urgently, 'Look—there's no need for you to do this. I can manage—really.'

'You don't like to be touched?'

'I've never thought about it.' She found herself startled into honesty.

'Then think now.' He paused, and there was a sudden harshness in his voice. 'Do you like to be in the arms of your lover?'

'Of course,' she said, and was glad that his head was bent, and that this time he could not look into her eyes and see that she was lying again.

She was expecting more questions, but he was suddenly silent, concentrating, presumably, on what he was doing.

There was disinfectant in the bowl that he'd brought, and Cressy tried not to wince as he swabbed the blister.

'What's that?' she asked dubiously as he uncapped a small pot of pale green ointment.

'It is made from herbs,' he said. 'It will help you to heal.'

When he'd finished, Cressy had a small, neat dressing held in place by a strip of plaster.

'*Efharisto,*' she said unwillingly. 'Thank you. It—it feels better already.'

'Good,' he said, getting to his feet. 'Then you will be able to dance with me tonight.'

'No,' Cressy said, feeling her heart thud painfully against her ribcage. 'No, I couldn't possibly.'

'Why not? Because your lover would not like it if he knew?'

'Perhaps.' Cressy examined her plaster with renewed interest. This non-existent boyfriend was proving useful, she thought. She had a dress ring in her luggage at the hotel. From now on she would wear it—on her engagement finger.

'Then why is he not here with you—making sure that no other man's hand touches his woman?'

She shrugged. 'He didn't want to come. He—he doesn't like very hot weather.'

'He has ice in his veins—this Englishman.' The harshness in his tone was inlaid with contempt.

'On the contrary.' Cressy moved her foot cautiously. 'But we have a modern relationship, *kyrie*. We don't have to spend every minute of every day together. We—like our space.'

He said slowly, 'If you belonged to me, *matia mou*, I would not let you out of my sight.'

She raised her eyebrows. 'Isn't that a little primitive?'

'Perhaps.' His mouth smiled but the agate eyes were oddly hard. 'But it is also—effective.'

He picked up the bowl and the roll of plaster. 'Come down when you are ready, *thespinis*. Yannis is waiting to cook your dinner.'

'I can't come down,' she said. 'I have nothing to wear.'

Draco indicated the dress that was lying on the bed. 'You call this nothing? Maria has put it here for you. It would honour her for you to wear it. And be an honour for you, too,' he added sharply. 'It was her wedding dress.'

'Oh.' Cressy swallowed. 'I had no idea. Then of course I must…' Her voice tailed away.

He replaced the dress carefully, then went to the door.

He said, 'I will tell them to expect you—to dine, and then to dance.'

And was gone.

Maria must have been very much slimmer at the time of her marriage, Cressy reflected, for the dress was almost a perfect fit.

Of course, the canvas shoes didn't really do it justice, but they'd have to suffice.

She'd brushed her damp hair until it hung, sleek and shining, to her shoulders, and applied a touch of colour to her mouth.

Now, she circled doubtfully in front of the long narrow mirror fixed to the wall. No one at her City office would have recognised her, she thought. She hardly recognised herself.

I look about seventeen, she thought. Except that I never looked like this when I was seventeen.

It wasn't just the dress. There was something in her face—something soft, almost wistful, that was new and unfamiliar. Under their fringe of lashes, her eyes were dreaming.

My eyes. That was what he had called her. Matia mou.

Only she wasn't going to think about that any more— what he'd said, or done. She was going to eat her meal, get on her ferry, and go back to the sanctuary of her expensive hotel. And if he turned up there, Security would know how to deal with him.

She nodded fiercely, and went down to the courtyard of the taverna.

Yannis welcomed her with extravagant admiration, and Maria appeared in the kitchen doorway, smiling mistily.

But Draco, as a cautious glance round soon revealed, was nowhere to be seen.

Perhaps the mention of a boyfriend had produced the desired result, Cressy told herself, firmly quashing an unwelcome tingle of disappointment.

To her surprise, the taverna was busy, and not just with local people. One of the tour companies had brought a crowd over from Alakos, it seemed, and most of the tables had been rearranged in a long line under the striped awning, and people, laughing and talking, were taking their seats there.

Yannis took Cressy to a secluded corner, protected by latticework screens covered, in turn, by a flowering vine.

He brought her ouzo, followed by dishes of taramasalata and houmous, and juicy black olives, with a platter of fresh bread.

As she sampled them, Cressy saw that a group of bouzouki players had arrived and were tuning their instruments.

For the dancing, thought Cressy with sudden unease. She sent a restive glance at her watch.

'There is a problem?' No mistaking that deep voice. Cressy looked up, shocked, to see Draco depositing a bottle of white wine on the table and taking the seat opposite.

Her warning antennae had let her down badly this time, she thought, biting her lip.

She hurried into speech. 'I was wondering about the ferry. What time does it leave?'

He sent an amused glance at the exuberant holidaymakers. 'When these people are ready to go. There is no hurry.' He paused. 'Or are you so anxious to leave us?'

She kept her voice even. 'I think it's time that I got back to the real world.'

'Or what passes for reality at the Hellenic Imperial hotel,' he said softly.

'You don't approve of such places?'

He shrugged. 'The islands need tourists, and tourists need hotels. They can prove—lucrative.'

'Especially,' Cressy said waspishly, 'for someone like you.'

His grin was unabashed. 'I do not deny it.' He picked up her glass to fill it with wine.

She said, 'I didn't order that.'

He smiled at her. 'It is a gift.'

'I didn't expect that either.'

'You ask for so little, *matia mou*. It is one of your many charms.'

Cressy flushed. 'If you really want to do me a favour, *kyrie*, you'll stop calling me *matia mou*.'

His brows lifted. 'Why?'

'Because it's— inappropriate. In my country it could be construed as harassment.'

She couldn't believe how prim and humourless she sounded.

He said quietly, 'But you are in my country now. On my island. And things are different here.'

'Is that a warning?' She stiffened.

'Do you feel that you are in danger?'

Yes, she wanted to scream. Yes—and I don't understand what's happening to me. I don't want this.

Aloud, she said lightly, 'I'm the stranger within your gates, *kyrie*. Isn't that what you told me? I've eaten your bread, and now I'm drinking your wine.' She lifted her glass towards him, then took a mouthful. It was cool and crisp against her dry throat. 'So why should I be afraid?'

He raised his own glass. '*Stin iyia sas.* To you, *thespinis*, and to your beauty in that dress. If your lover was here, he would beg on his knees to make you his bride.' He drank, and put down his glass.

He said softly, his gaze holding hers, 'I will make a bargain with you. I will not call you ''my eyes'' until

your eyes promise me that I may. And, in return, you
will tell me your given name.'

Under the cool white cotton, her skin felt as if it was
on fire.

She lifted her chin. 'Very well, *kyrie*. I'm called
Cressida.'

'Cressida,' he repeated thoughtfully. 'The golden
one—who was faithless to her lover Troilus.'

'According to Shakespeare, and the other men who
wrote about her,' Cressy said crisply. 'She, of course,
might have had a different viewpoint. And, if it comes
to that, your own namesake isn't much to brag about—
a tyrant imposing laws that no one could live under.
Although that shouldn't surprise me,' she added with
warmth.

'Quarrelling?' Yannis arrived with two plates of
grilled swordfish, Greek salads, and a big bowl of fries.
'Not while you eat my food, or you will get bad stom-
achs.' He wagged an admonishing finger at them both,
and went off.

Draco grinned at her. 'He is right. Let us begin
again.'

He held out his hand. '*Hero poli*, Cressida. I am
pleased to meet you.'

Reluctantly, she allowed her fingers to be enclosed in
the warmth of his. '*Hero poli*—Draco.'

'And your name is very beautiful,' he added.

Cressy wrinkled her nose. 'I used to hate it,' she con-
fessed. 'But then I hated everything about being a girl.
I wanted so badly to be a boy when I was little that my
father used to call me Sid as a joke. My mother was
very cross about it, so he'd never use it in front of her.
Only when we were on our own.'

'And does he still call you—Sid?' His brows lifted.

Cressy looked down at her plate. 'Not for a long time,' she said quietly.

'I am not surprised.' He gave a faint smile. 'I must tell you, Cressida, that you are no boy.'

She met the sudden intensity of the dark eyes and flushed, reaching hurriedly for her knife and fork.

The swordfish was succulent and delicious, and she ate every scrap, even conducting a laughing battle with Draco over the last few fries.

'It is good to meet a woman who does not wish to starve herself,' he told her as he refilled her glass.

She shook her head. 'One of these days all these calories will suddenly explode, and I'll turn into a mountain.'

'No.' The dark eyes travelled over her in smiling, sensuous appraisal. 'For me, you will always look as you do now, *agapi mou.*'

Cressy frowned. 'What does that mean?' she asked suspiciously.

He laughed. 'It is best that you don't know.'

Cressy felt her colour deepen helplessly. To cover her confusion, she turned to watch the bouzouki players, tapping her fingers on the table to the music.

Draco was watching her. 'You like bouzouki?'

'I don't know very much,' she admitted. 'Just "Zorba's Dance", like everyone else.' She hesitated. 'I liked what you were dancing to this morning.'

'That was also by Theodorakis.' He smiled faintly. 'He is still very much a hero. A man whose music spoke to the people.'

She said, 'I—I hope you're going to dance tonight.'

'Only if you will promise, just once, to be my partner.'

'But I couldn't,' Cressy protested. 'I've never done any Greek dancing.'

'I did not mean that. When the entertainment is over, Yannis plays other music.' The agate eyes glittered at her. 'We will choose something very slow—very sweet—so that you won't hurt your foot.'

'Oh.' Cressy felt hollow inside, but she mustered a smile. 'Thank you.'

'Would you like some dessert? Halva, perhaps—or baklava?'

'Just coffee, please.'

He said, 'I'll fetch it.'

She watched him lithely threading his way between the tables, and saw without surprise that several of the woman holidaymakers from the large party were watching him too, nudging each other and exchanging whispered comments and giggles.

I could always send a note over saying, 'He's available,' Cressy thought sourly. Only people might get killed in the rush.

She'd come away on holiday to relax, yet she'd never felt so edgy and restless in her life.

She'd had her day and her evening neatly planned, but here she was, in another woman's wedding dress, having dinner with a man who supplemented his income by 'befriending' lonely women.

And she wasn't lonely, she told herself vehemently. Yes, she missed her father's company, but she had plenty of friends. She could go out every night, if she wanted. And there were plenty of men who'd be keen to escort her.

Which was fine. It was when they tried to get closer that warning bells started to ring and she felt herself freeze.

No man was prepared to be held at arm's length for ever. She understood that perfectly well. She'd always assumed that one of her casual friendships would eventually bloom into something deeper. Something based on liking and respect, rather than casual physical attraction.

She'd always sworn she'd never be caught in that trap.

So a holiday romance had never been on the cards.

Draco was good-looking, with a sexual aura as powerful as a force field, but this time he'd chosen the wrong target, she told herself with determination.

Their acquaintance would end with dinner, as she would make clear.

I'll pay Yannis for the meal, she thought, and ask him to tell Draco goodbye for me.

And then she'd never set foot on Myros again. She would arrange for the hotel to launder and return Maria's dress and collect her own things. And that would be an end to it.

She looked round for Yannis, but at the same moment the bouzouki players struck up again, and she saw that he and three other men had formed a line and begun to dance, their hands resting on each other's shoulders. It was a slow, intricate dance, but their movements were perfectly synchronised, and strangely dignified, Cressy thought, watching, entranced.

This wasn't just a cabaret act, as it was at the hotel, she realised as she joined the rest of the audience in clapping in time to the music. These were men to whom their own culture was a living, breathing thing.

The music quickened its pace. The dance changed to include Maria and a couple of other women, and, gradually, the crowd from Alakos were persuaded to join in too, weaving their way between the tables in a long, twirling chain.

A waiter appeared at her side with coffee. 'For you, *thespinis*. Kyrios Draco says he is to dance next.'

Giving her an ideal chance to slip away, thought Cressy. As the waiter moved off, she stopped him. '*O logariasimos, parakolo?*' Adding, 'May I have the bill, please?' in case he didn't understand her attempt at Greek.

But he didn't seem to have much grasp of English either, because he shrugged, smilingly spread his hands, and kept on walking.

The dance finished and everyone sat down, laughing and talking.

When the music started again, it was slow and haunting, almost plaintive.

Cressy knew that Draco had appeared, because the chattering voices were stilled suddenly, and there was a new tension in the air. She stared down at her coffee, not wanting to look up—not wanting to watch, but eventually impelled to.

Across the distance that divided them, above the heads of the crowd, his eyes met hers—held them steadily. He inclined his head in silent acknowledgement. Then he began to dance.

Yannis and the other men knelt in a half-circle around him, clapping the rhythm. Tonight, there was none of the exuberance she'd seen that morning. The movements were as passionate, but they spoke of pain and isolation. The music seemed to wail and weep, emphasising the yearning expressed by his taut body.

Cressy, totally enthralled, saw weariness and suffering. And every so often a dangerous flicker of wildness.

She thought, with an odd certainty, This is about love—and the loss of love...

When it stopped, there was silence for a moment, and then the applause broke out, wave after wave of it, and people were standing to take photographs.

When disco music began to play over the sound system it was almost a shock. But no one else could have followed Draco, she thought.

Everyone was up on their feet, joining in, jigging around vigorously. Glad, she thought, to dispel some of the emotion of the last few minutes.

Cressy noticed the girl at once. She was red-haired and pretty, wearing a tiny Lycra skirt and a skimpy top displaying a generous amount of cleavage. Her hand was on Draco's arm and she was smiling up at him, moving closer, her whole body an invitation.

Cressy put down her coffee cup, aware that her hand was shaking. She knew an overwhelming impulse to rush over to them—to drag the redhead away—to slap her—scratch her nails down that simpering face.

But she wasn't a violent person, she told herself vehemently. She never had been.

Except that she'd never been jealous before. And that made all the difference.

The resentment she felt for Eloise didn't even feature on the same scale, she thought, closing her eyes, conscious that she felt slightly sick.

She and Draco came from two different worlds. So how could she possibly feel these things for a total stranger—someone she didn't want? That she couldn't want...

The soundtrack had changed to something soft and dreamy, and Cressy kept her eyes shut, because she didn't want to see the red-haired girl in Draco's arms.

His voice, soft and amused, said, 'It is too soon to sleep, *agapi mou*. You have a bargain to keep.'

She looked up at him, feeling her stomach muscles clench in unwelcome excitement and longing.

She said coolly, 'Shouldn't you be spending time with your adoring public?'

His grin was appreciative. 'She was beautiful, *ne*?' He whistled. 'Such a mouth—such breasts.' Lazily, he scanned Cressy's indignantly parted lips, then let his gaze travel slowly downwards. That was all he did, yet for one dizzy, scared moment she knew how his mouth would feel on hers—recognised the intimate touch of his hands on her body.

He went on quietly, 'But I am here with you, my golden one, so don't disappoint me.'

He held out his hand, and, silently, she rose from her seat and went with him. Felt his arms close round her, drawing her against him. Cressy surrendered, sliding her own arms round his firm waist and resting her cheek against his chest as they moved quietly together to the music, one tune fading effortlessly into another.

She was not an accomplished dancer, yet in Draco's arms she seemed to drift in perfect attunement, as if she was part of him. It might have been a dream, except that she was only too aware of the physical reality of his nearness.

She was trembling inside, her body tingling as the warmth of his skin invaded her thin layers of clothing, giving her the helpless impression that she was naked in his arms. Shocking her by the sudden scalding heat of desire.

There were no pretences anymore. He was as aroused as she was.

He whispered against her ear, his voice raw and urgent, 'You feel it too, *ne*, my girl, my heaven? This need we have for each other?'

She pulled away, staring up at him, her eyes wide, the pupils dilated as she met the glint of golden fire in his.

She said hoarsely, 'I—I can't do this. I have to go—have to...'

And stopped, as she realised they were alone. The courtyard was deserted. Yannis and his helpers had vanished into the taverna, the glass doors discreetly closed behind them, and the crowd from Alakos had gone.

She said on a little sob, 'The ferry—oh, God, the ferry...'

She ran out of the courtyard and down the street towards the harbour, but Draco caught her before she'd gone more than a few yards.

'The ferry has gone,' he said.

'But you knew I had to catch it. You knew that.' Her voice shook. 'Now I'm stranded. Oh, *hell*. What am I going to do?'

'You stay here,' he said calmly. 'It's not a problem.'

'Yes,' she said bitterly. 'Oh, yes, it is. You don't understand...'

'I know more than you think.' He put his hands on her shoulders, looking down into her angry, frightened face. 'You believe I have kept you here to share my bed tonight, but you are wrong. I shall sleep at my own house, and you will stay here with Yannis and Maria.'

Cressy gasped. 'When was this decided?'

'When we realised that there would be no room for you on the ferry. An overcrowded boat is not safe, particularly when many of the passengers have been drinking Metaxa. It is better to wait for tomorrow.'

She bit her lip. 'Very well.' She paused. 'But the hotel. They'll know I haven't come back...'

'Yannis has telephoned them, so all is well.'

She said quietly, 'Then there's nothing left to say.'

The music had stopped when they came back to the courtyard, and the lights were out.

Draco walked beside her, his tread as quiet as a cat's. He did not touch her, but she felt him in every fibre of her being.

He would kiss her, she thought confusedly, and she wanted him to. In fact, she ached for him. But she'd betrayed too much already, while they were dancing. And when his mouth touched hers she would have no defences left.

No strength to say no when he walked up the moonlit stairs beside her to the quiet, cool room with the wide bed. No power to resist when he drew her down into his arms.

His for the taking, she thought. And he would know that, and would take...

They reached the foot of the stone steps and she paused uncertainly, waiting for him to reach for her.

He said softly, 'Until tomorrow—Cressida the golden. But now—*kalinichta*. Goodnight.' And she felt the brush of his lips against her hair, as swift and tantalising as a butterfly's wing.

And then she was free, walking up the stairs alone, and bewildered. She turned at the top of the stairs and looked down at him, the still shadow waiting there. Watching her go.

She said huskily, 'I don't understand. What do you want from me?'

'I want everything, *agapi mou*.' There was a strange

harshness in his voice. 'All you have to give. And nothing less will do.' He paused. 'But I can wait.'

He turned away into the darkness, leaving Cressy standing motionless, her hand pressed to her trembling mouth.

CHAPTER FIVE

'MISS FIELDING—are you all right?'

Cressida started violently, and looked up to see one of the senior nurses standing beside her.

'Yes,' she said. 'I'm fine. I'm sorry—I was miles away.'

A thousand miles, she thought, and another world...

'I'm going to ask you to go to the visitors' room for a little while. The consultant is coming to see your father, and he'll talk to you afterwards.'

'Of course.' She almost stumbled up from her chair and along the corridor. It wasn't a comfortable room. There was a table in the middle of the room with magazines, and a few moulded plastic chairs ranged round the walls.

She went over to the window and looked out at a vista of rooftops.

She felt ashamed. She was supposed to be here for her father, trying to infuse him with her own youth and strength, and instead she'd allowed herself to daydream—to remember things far better forgotten. A time that was past and done with.

Except...

The memory of that enigmatic e-mail message would not be so easily dismissed.

I am waiting for you.

It can't be him, she denied, almost violently. I won't believe it.

She grabbed a magazine from the table and sat down,

only to open it at a page recommending Greek holidays. She looked at the crescent of bleached sand fringed by turquoise water in the picture and realised bleakly that there was no refuge from her memories.

They crowded her mind, filling it. Drawing her inexorably back to Myros.

She'd hardly slept that first night at the taverna. She had been too aware of the danger threatening her to be able to relax. And Draco was the most danger she'd ever encountered in her life.

No wonder he was a fisherman, she had thought, turning over restlessly and thumping the flat pillow with her fist. He knew exactly how to keep a woman hooked and helpless.

But he wouldn't reel her in. She wouldn't allow it to happen. She was her own person, and her plan didn't include casual sex. It never had.

Draco had to learn that no matter how attractive he might be he was not always going to win.

And he'd soon find consolation. Every time he danced there'd be a queue of eager and willing girls vying for his attention. He wouldn't have time to remember the one that got away.

She had nodded fiercely, and closed her eyes with determination.

When she'd awoken, early sun had been spilling through the slats in the shutters across the tiled floor.

The first thing she had seen was that all the things she'd used yesterday, including the beach towel, were lying pristinely laundered and neatly folded on the chair, and the white dress, which had been carefully draped there, had gone. Maria, it seemed, had performed a dawn raid.

Which I didn't intend, Cressy had thought, as she slid out of bed and headed for the shower.

When she had gone down the outside stairs, Maria had been sweeping the courtyard. To Cressy's embarrassment, it had been made immediately clear that she would be allowed to pay nothing for her night's lodging or her meal. Nor would she be permitted to have the white dress cleaned.

'It is my pleasure to do this for you,' Maria declared. 'Everyone say how beautiful you look in the dress.'

Cressy flushed a little. 'Oh?'

'Ah, yes.' Maria gave her a roguish look. 'And one person in particular, *ne*?' She pointed to the table Cressy had occupied the night before. 'Sit there, *kyria*, and I will bring you breakfast. Rolls and coffee, and some of the honey from my sister's bees.' She bustled off, leaving Cressy to take a careful look around, but she had the courtyard to herself, she realised with relief.

She consulted the list of ferry times in her bag, and saw that the first one ran in just over half an hour. She should make it easily.

Her meal also included fresh orange juice and a bowl of creamy yoghurt. By the time she got up from the table she was replete.

'I can't thank you enough,' she told Yannis and Maria when they came to say goodbye to her.

'You are welcome.' Yannis's hand closed over hers. 'Welcome at any time. Your room will always be waiting.'

Cressy's smile was a little taut. 'Maybe—one day,' she said. She hesitated. 'And please would you thank Draco for me? He's been—kind.'

She picked up her bag and headed down to the harbour, determined to be the first one on the ferry. But it wasn't moored at the landing point she'd used yesterday. In fact she couldn't see it anywhere, she realised frantically, shading her eyes and staring out to sea.

'So you did not intend to say goodbye.' Draco got up from the stack of wooden crates he'd been sitting on. The shorts he was wearing were just as disreputable as the previous pair, and he'd topped them with an unbuttoned white cotton shirt.

Cressy lifted her chin. 'I—I left a message with Maria.'

'Now you can give it to me in person.'

Exactly what she hadn't wanted. She said stiltedly, 'Just—thank you, and good luck.'

'I believe in fate more than luck.' He looked her over, smiling faintly. 'Last night you were Cressida,' he said. 'But today you are Sid again. What will you be tomorrow, *agapi mou*?'

She shook her head. She said, almost inaudibly. 'I don't think I know any more.'

'Perhaps you are being reborn,' he said. 'Rising like a phoenix from the ashes of your former life.'

She threw back her head. 'But I don't want that. I'm quite content with things as they are.'

'Content?' There was scorn in his voice. 'Is that the most you can wish for? What a small, narrow word, when there is excitement, passion and rapture to be experienced.'

'Perhaps,' she said, 'I like to feel safe.'

'There is no safety, *agapi mou*. Not in life. Not in love. As you will discover when you stop running away.' He shrugged. 'But if you wish to return to Alakos and the comfort of your hotel, I will take you.'

'Thank you,' she said. 'But I'll wait for the proper ferry.'

'Then you'll wait a long time,' he said drily. 'Kostas drank too much Metaxa last night on Alakos. There will be no ferry until tonight.'

Cressy gasped indignantly. 'Is he allowed to do that?'

Draco grinned. 'He does not usually wait for permission. It is my boat or nothing, *pethi mou*.'

She gave him a fulminating glance, then sighed. 'All right. Your boat. Just as long as I get back to Alakos.'

'Why the hurry? Are you so sure that Myros has nothing more to offer?' There was an undercurrent of mockery in his tone.

'I'm paying to stay at the Hellenic Imperial,' she reminded him tautly.

'Ah, money,' he said. 'That concerns you deeply?'

'I like to get my money's worth. But I'm sure you're far above such considerations.'

He lifted a negligent shoulder. 'It's easier not to think about it, I promise you.'

Cressy bit her lip, aware that she'd been ungracious about his undoubted poverty.

She said, 'You must let me pay you for the trip.'

He sent her a quizzical look. 'Did Yannis and Maria ask you to pay for the meal last night—or your room?'

'No,' she said. 'They didn't. But...'

'And I am no different. There is no charge.' And there was a note in his voice which told her not to argue.

She sat tensely in the bow as the caique pushed its way through the sparkling sunlit water. The faint early haze was clearing and it was going to be another scorching day, she thought, lifting her hair away from the nape of her neck.

Draco said from the tiller, 'You are too warm? There is an awning...'

'No, I'm fine,' she assured him quickly. 'It's just so—beautiful.'

'I think you are falling in love, *agapi mou*, with my country. You will never want to go home.'

She stared at the horizon. 'I think my boss would have something to say about that.'

'You are indispensable?'

'Hardly. I don't think anyone really is. We just fool ourselves, then we go, and our space is filled, and no one even remembers we were once there.'

'That is a sad thought for such a lovely day,' Draco said after a pause. 'But you will be remembered always.'

She shook her head. 'I don't think so.'

'Ah, but you will,' he said. 'By your lover, for one—and your father, for another. And I—I will remember too.'

'You will?' She sent him a look of disbelief. 'That's nonsense.'

'Of course I'll remember. It is not every day I meet a girl with hair like the sun, and moonlight in her eyes, who is called Sid.'

Her heart twisted slowly and painfully. To cover the sudden emotion, she pulled a face. 'I knew I'd regret mentioning that.'

'There is nothing to regret. It is good that your father had this special name for you.' He smiled at her. 'Sometimes when I look at you I can see the little girl you were.'

Cressy turned away and stared at the sea. She said flatly, 'She's been gone a long time.'

'You will find her again when you hold your own daughter in your arms.'

How simple he made it sound, Cressy thought, her throat aching. And how unlikely it really was.

She straightened her shoulders. 'Alakos doesn't seem to be coming any closer.'

He said, 'I thought you would wish to pay a last visit to our beach.'

'And I thought I'd made it clear I wanted to go straight back.' There was sudden ice in her voice as she turned on him, but Draco did not appear chilled.

His eyes met hers steadily. 'You offered to pay for your trip. This is the price—that you swim with me just once.'

She said acidly, 'Dancing last night. Swimming today. Do you set up a full fitness programme for all your women?'

He spoke very quietly. 'That is a suggestion that demeans us both. But if it is really what you think, then there is no more to be said.'

She watched him move the tiller, heading the caique out into the open sea.

Then she looked back at the horizon and found it suddenly blurred with unshed tears.

It was a miserably silent journey. To Cressy's surprise, Draco avoided the main harbour and sailed round to the hotel's private bay, bringing his craft skilfully alongside the small jetty.

In a subdued voice, she said, 'I don't think you're meant to be here.'

He shrugged. 'Does it matter? I shall soon be gone.'

His touch completely impersonal, he helped her ashore, and put her bag on the planking beside her.

She said in a sudden rush, 'Draco—I'm sorry—I didn't mean what I said. I—I don't want us to part bad friends, but I'm just so confused. I can't seem to get my head together...'

He nodded, but the bronze face showed no sign of softening.

'Then start listening to your heart instead, Cressida. And when you do, you know where to find me.' He pointed towards Myros. 'I shall be there—waiting for you.'

She stood on the jetty and watched until the boat was a mere speck, but he never looked back.

Cressy jumped as the door to the visitors' room opened and the consultant came in.

'Miss Fielding.' His handshake was limp for such an eminent man. 'You'll be pleased to hear that your father is making good progress. If it continues, we should be able to send him home next week.'

'Oh.' Cressy sat down on one of the uncomfortable chairs. 'Oh, that's such a relief. And the operation?'

'As soon as we consider he's fit enough.' The consultant looked vaguely round. 'Is your mother not here? I should speak to her about his future care.'

Cressy said evenly, 'My stepmother is—away.'

'Of course,' he said. 'Building up her strength to nurse the invalid at home, no doubt. Admirable.'

Cressida bent her head. 'Now may I go back to my father, please?

'You're going to be all right, Dad,' she whispered to the still figure in the bed. 'Isn't that wonderful news? I just wish you'd give some sign that you can hear me. Although I do understand that you've got to rest.

'And I can work for you, Daddy. I can deal with the bank, and the mortgage company, and everyone. I can't get your money back, but maybe I can stop you losing everything else. I'll talk to them—I'll make them listen. Because I need to work—to stop me from thinking. Remembering...'

In spite of the heat, she shivered.

She had gone straight up to the hotel, she recalled, and lain down on the bed in her air-conditioned room and stared up at the ceiling...

There was a vast, aching emptiness inside her. A trembling, frightened nothingness.

She thought, What am I doing? What have I done?

Draco's face seemed to float above her, and she closed her eyes to shut him out. But she couldn't dismiss her other senses so easily. Her skin burned as she remembered the sensuous pressure of his body against hers. She seemed to breathe the scent of him. To feel the brush of his lips on her flesh.

A little moan escaped her. She was consumed by bewildered longing, her body torn apart by physical needs that she'd never known before.

She twisted restlessly on the bed, trying to find peace and calm, but failing.

She got up and went out on to the balcony, but the indigo shimmer of Myros on the horizon drove her inside again.

She stayed in her room until midday, when she made herself go down and join the queue at the lavish buffet on the hotel's terrace.

She'd never realised before how many couples seemed to be staying at the hotel, wandering around hand in hand, or with their arms round each other.

Making her blindingly—piercingly aware of her own isolation—her own loneliness.

Making her realise that she couldn't bear it any

longer. And that she didn't have to—that she too could choose to be happy for a little while.

A few days—even a few hours, she thought. I'd settle for that. Whatever the ultimate cost.

She could tell herself a thousand times that she was crazy even to contemplate such a thing, but it made no difference. Her will power—her control didn't seem to matter any more. The ache of yearning was too strong, too compelling, and it was drawing her back.

When she told them at Reception that she was going back to Myros to stay for a while she half expected they would try to dissuade her, but her decision was accepted almost casually.

Down at the harbour, she didn't wait for the ferry, but paid one of the local boatmen to take her across to the other island.

She was trembling as she walked up from the quay towards the taverna. This was madness, and she knew it, and it would serve her right if she walked in and found Draco with someone else, she thought, pain twisting inside her. But one swift glance told her that he wasn't there.

Yannis was playing *tavli*, and his jaw dropped when he saw her. Then he recovered himself, and got to his feet smiling broadly.

The *thespinis* was welcome. It was good that she had come back. Especially as he had mended the wheel on his sister's bicycle.

Up in her room, Cressy changed into a black bikini, topping it with a scooped neck T-shirt in the same colour and a wrapround skirt in a black and white swirling print.

All the way to the beach she was straining her ears to hear music, but there was only silence and solitude.

She left the bicycle on the clifftop and scrambled down to the sand. The heat was intense, but she felt cold with disappointment.

She had been so ridiculously sure that he'd be there— waiting for her.

Was it really only twenty-four hours? she wondered, spreading her towel in the same spot. It seemed more like a year.

She slipped off her skirt and top, kicked off her sandals, and ran down to the sea, welcoming its cool caress against her overheated skin.

She needed to work off some of this emotion somehow, and a long, strenuous swim would do the trick. If only it could restore her common sense at the same time.

She drove herself on, pounding up and down as if she was covering lengths in a pool, until her arms and legs were heavy with tiredness and she knew it was time to go back.

She put a foot down, finding sand and shingle, and began to wade towards the beach, wringing the excess water out of her hair.

Out of the dazzle of the sun she saw him, standing motionless on the edge of the sea, small waves curling round his bare feet.

She began to run, cursing the pressure of the water which held her back.

He was holding her towel, she realised, and as she reached him he wrapped it round her, pulling her into his arms. She lifted her face mutely, and for the first time experienced the hungry demand of his mouth on hers.

The kiss seemed to last an eternity, as if, with that first taste, they could not get enough of each other.

He was not gentle, nor did she require him to be. His mouth clung, burned, tore at hers as if he was trying to absorb her into his being.

Her own lips parted breathlessly, welcoming the thrust of his tongue, inciting the dark, heated exploration to go deeper still. Offering herself without reserve.

Sun, sea and bleached sand were performing a crazy, spinning dance around her, and she put up her hands to grip his bare shoulders. She was trembling under this wild onslaught on her senses, her legs shaking under her.

Just as she thought she might collapse on the sand at his feet, Draco lifted her into his arms and carried her up the beach. He'd spread a rug in the shadow of some rocks and he lowered her on to it, coming down beside her, seeking her mouth again, his hand tangling in her damp blonde hair.

She surrendered her lips eagerly to the sensuous rapture of his possession. She felt as if she was drunk—or that she'd entered some other undreamed of dimension.

Her hands caressed his back, holding him to her as his mouth travelled downwards, questing the curve of her throat and the small hollows at its base.

His tongue found the cleft between her breasts and lingered, and she gasped, her body arching involuntarily, her nipples hardening in excitement under the damp fabric.

His lips brushed each soft swell of flesh above the confines of the bikini top as one hand stroked down her body to find and cup the delicate contour of her hip with total mastery. Making no secret of his intention.

He lifted his head and stared down at her, the dark eyes slumbrous, a flush of deeper colour along the high cheekbones, as if he was waiting for some sign from her.

Watching him, Cressy raised a hand and undid the halter strap of her bikini, then released the little clip, freeing the tiny garment completely.

Draco bent his head and with great precision took it from her with his teeth.

He tossed it aside and lowered his mouth fully to her bare breasts, paying them slow and languorous homage, his lips moulding their soft fullness. As she felt the provocative flicker of his tongue across the puckered rose of her nipples a little moan of surprise and longing escaped her.

His mouth enclosed each hot, excited peak in turn, pleasuring them softly and subtly. Eyes closed, Cressy gave herself up to delight, feeling her last remaining inhibitions sliding away.

At the same time his fingers were feathering across her thighs, brushing the delicate mound they guarded, and her body responded with a rush of scalding, passionate heat.

His mouth moved down her body slowly, almost druggingly, paying minute attention to each curve and hollow. He murmured softly in his own language, resting his cheek against the concavity of her stomach.

She was dimly aware that at some point he had discarded the swimming trunks that were his sole covering, but it was only when she felt the glide of his fingers against the heated, throbbing core of her womanhood that she realised that she too was now naked.

He kissed her mouth again, his tongue teasing hers as his hands continued their gentle erotic play, taking her ever closer to some brink she'd never known existed.

As her breathing quickened she felt him move slightly, his body covering hers, his hands sliding under her to lift her for his possession.

For a fleeting moment she experienced the heated pressure of him against her, seeking her. And then there was pain, and she heard her voice, muffled against his shoulder, crying out in shock and sudden panic.

He was instantly still. Then he rolled away from her almost frantically, his breath rasping in his throat.

When she dared look, he was sitting a few feet away, one leg drawn up, his forehead resting on his knee. There was a faint sheen of perspiration gleaming on his skin, and his chest heaved as he fought for control.

She whispered his name, and when there was no response reached across and put her hand lightly on his arm.

He shook her off almost violently. His voice was a snarl. 'Do not touch me. It is not safe.'

She said in a whisper, 'What is it? I don't understand…'

As the silence lengthened between them she said, more urgently, her voice shaking a little, 'Talk to me, please. Tell me what's wrong. What I've done.'

Draco turned and looked at her, his dark eyes hooded, the firm mouth compressed.

He said, 'You have done nothing wrong. The mistake, God help us both, is mine.'

He reached for his trunks and pulled them on, his face taut.

Colour stormed into her face and she grabbed clumsily for her towel, holding it in front of her defensively, just as if there was an inch of her that he'd left undiscovered.

'You lied to me, Cressida. Why?' His voice was harsh.

'Lied?' she repeated uncomprehendingly.

'You let me think you had a lover. But it is not true. So why did you pretend.'

'What did you expect me to do?' Her eyes blurred with humiliated tears. 'It was what you wanted to hear—wasn't it? And it seemed—safer.'

'No,' he said. 'It was not safe. It was a stupid lie, and a dangerous one. You thought I would not know?'

She bent her head. 'I—I didn't think so. I didn't realise it would make any difference...'

She heard him whisper something sharp and violent, then he was beside her again. He drew her towards him, cupping her face gently between his hands, making her meet his searching gaze.

He said quietly, 'It makes all the difference in the world, *agapi mou*. But I am also to blame. I should have realised that you were claiming a sophistication you did not possess.'

She said tautly, 'Of course, you know so much about women.'

'More than you know of men, certainly.'

Cressy bit her lip, unable to deny his curt response. Her voice shook slightly. 'Draco—I'm so sorry...'

'Sorry?' he repeated, his voice incredulous. 'You offer me the ultimate gift—and say you are sorry?'

She said flatly, 'But it's a gift you don't seem to want.'

His mouth relaxed into the shadow of a smile. 'You think I don't want you, *agapi mou*?' He took her hands and carried them fleetingly to his body. 'You are wrong. But a woman's innocence should not be thrown away to feed the hunger of the moment. You deserve better.'

His lips touched hers, swiftly and gently. 'Now dress yourself, and we will go back to the town, where there are more people and less temptations.'

He got to his feet and walked down the beach, where he stood, his back turned, gazing at the sea, while Cressy huddled into her clothing.

When he came back to her, she said, 'I think I'd better go back to Alakos.'

'Why should you do that?' His dark brows drew into a frown.

'Because I'm very embarrassed.' She made a business of folding her towel. 'I've made a real fool of myself.' She added carefully, 'And I'd just be in the way if I stayed.'

'Ah,' Draco said softly. 'You feel you might hinder my search for the next willing body.' He cast a despairing look at the heavens. 'Is that truly what you think of me?'

She said, 'Draco—I don't know what to think. I don't *know* you.'

'Then why did you come back?' He spoke gently, but there was an inflexible note in his voice. 'Just so that I could rid you of your unwanted virginity? I don't believe that.'

She bit her lip. 'Because I found I couldn't stay away. And now I've ruined everything.'

He sighed. 'Nothing is spoiled—unless you wish it to be.' There was a silence, then he stroked the curve of her face with one long finger. 'Is that what you want, *pethi mou*? Or shall we begin all over again? Start to learn about each other, not just with our bodies, but our minds?'

She said on a little sob, 'Oh, Draco, please.'

'Then so be it.' He took her hand, held it in his, his

fingers strong and warm. 'But understand, Cressida, that this changes everything. And if you leave me now, I shall follow. However long, however far.' He paused. 'You accept this?'

And, from some great distance, she heard herself answer, 'Yes.'

CHAPTER SIX

IT HAD just seemed a romantic thing to say on a beach, Cressy told herself as she drove home from the hospital. After all, they'd both known that their time together was going to be limited. That sooner or later the idyll would end, and she would fly back to real life.

What she hadn't foreseen was that it would indeed be much sooner.

At first, as the sunlit days had passed, she'd felt she was living in a dream, or under a spell that Draco had cast around her.

Most of her waking hours had been spent in his company, and even when she'd been asleep the image of him had never been far from her mind.

The first part of the morning she'd usually spent alone. She'd assumed that Draco was out in his boat, fishing, but when she'd mentioned this to Yannis he'd shrugged and said, 'I think he is at his house, Kyria Cressida. He is having some building done.'

Cressy understood. A lot of local houses seemed to be built in instalments, the owners occupying the ground floor until they could afford to add further storeys.

Draco had clearly made enough money to build another floor on to his, and if there was a vaguely troubling query at the back of her mind as to exactly where that money came from, she dismissed it. Nothing was allowed to impinge on her happiness.

Sometimes she wondered wistfully whether she

would ever be asked to see his house, but assumed it
would never happen. These close-knit village commu-
nities might not be pleased to see one of their number
with an *anglitha*, especially if he'd been earmarked for
one of their daughters, she thought with a pang.

Anyway, if Draco wished to keep his private life to
himself, that was his concern. He would have to go on
living here after she'd gone…

She sighed. The realisation that her time in Greece
was running out was causing her real pain.

I didn't really want to come here, she thought, grimacing. Now I don't want to leave.

It was hard to separate one day from another, when
all of them were touched with gold. Sometimes they
went out on the boat, landing on some quiet beach to
swim, and cook the fish they'd caught over a wood fire.

At other times Draco drove the pick-up to the island's
peaceful beauty spots, along the coast, or up into the
high bare hills. And at night they danced together.

She was relaxed with him now. They shared a lot of
laughter, but they could be quiet together too. When he
teased her, she teased back. They had, she thought, become friends—and that was good.

But she couldn't deny the painful, ecstatic lift of her
heart that happened each time he strode into the courtyard of the taverna to find her. Or the sweet, sensual
ache that any physical contact with him seemed to
evoke.

For much of the time he kept her at a distance, and
she knew it. Just sometimes, in the drowsy afternoons,
he would draw her into his arms and explore her mouth
gently with his. Her hair seemed to entrance him. 'Like
pale silk,' he would whisper, winding strands round his
fingers and carrying them to his lips.

But—so far and no further, it seemed. The merest touch of his lips could ignite her desire, making her burn and melt with longing for the intimacy of his touch, for the consummation that her aroused flesh had been denied, but if he was aware of that, he gave no sign.

Just once, when he'd kissed her goodnight, she'd tried to hold him, pressing herself against him, her lips parting in mute invitation beneath the pressure of his. Longing to spark the passion that she knew lay just beneath the surface.

But he'd gently detached her clinging hands and stepped back, bending his head to drop a kiss on each soft palm before he let her go. And she had walked away up the stairs, knowing that he would not follow.

His control seemed to be total—and yet there were occasional moments when she felt him watching her. Was aware of a strange tension quivering along her nerve-endings, as if her body had somehow discerned the naked hunger in his and was responding to it.

Someone else was watching her too, she thought. Maria. The older woman was still warmly friendly, but once or twice Cressy had caught an anxious glance, or a little worried frown, and she wondered why.

But not too deeply. Her only real concern was the moment when she would see Draco again—would hear his voice and feel his smile touch her own mouth.

And that was all that mattered.

She didn't realise, of course, how swiftly and how finally things could change.

She woke early that day on Myros, to the bleak realisation that there was just over a week of her holiday left. She sat up in bed, hugging her knees, frowning a little. Maybe this was the time to walk away—while she still could. Before she was in too deep and reduced to begging.

Draco had told her the previous evening that he would come for her just after breakfast.

'So for once you're not going to work on your house.' Cressy had raised her eyebrows. 'I'm honoured.' She'd paused. 'How's it getting on—the house, I mean?'

He had shrugged. 'It is almost finished. It has taken longer than I thought.'

She'd been tempted to say, I'd love to see it, simply to test his reaction, but she had remained silent.

When she considered, the house was the least of it. There were so many things she still didn't know about him, she thought, her frown deepening. He had never spoken of his family, or mentioned friends apart from the crowd at the taverna, and even there he seemed to be treated with a certain respect rather than the usual raucous camaraderie.

But then he was incurious about her background too, she acknowledged.

She knew all kinds of little details about him, of course. She knew that his lashes were long enough to curl on his cheek when he slept. That there was a scar on his thigh, a relic from his boyhood when he'd gashed himself on a rock while swimming.

She was also aware that he could only relax for a certain time before he became restive, and that he secretly preferred her to wear dresses rather than trousers.

There'd been times recently, too, when he'd appeared to retreat so deeply into his own thoughts that it had been impossible for her to reach him, and this had made her feel oddly helpless and a little on edge.

Perhaps he was trying to find a humane way of telling

her that it was over and suggesting she went back to
Alakos, she thought desolately as she went to her
shower.

'Today we'll do something different,' he told her as
they walked down to the harbour. 'There is something
I want you to see.'

She felt a little surge of pleasure. Maybe at last she
was going to see the mysterious house—or even meet
his family.

She said lightly, 'That sounds intriguing.'

They sailed past their usual beach, heading north.

'Where are we going?'

'You have never been all round the island. I think
you should.' Draco gave her the tiller.

'Oh.' Cressy masked her disappointment. After a moment, she said slowly, 'Myros is so lovely, Draco. It's
like part of a different world. I—I shall hate to say
goodbye.'

'So enjoy it while you can,' he said casually. 'And
don't run us on to the rocks, *pethi mou*.'

To the north of the island the coastline became more
dramatic, with one high promontory standing out from
the rest. And on this jutting headland, clinging to it like
a lizard on a rock, was the massive sprawl of a villa,
white-walled and roofed in terracotta.

'My God.' Cressy shaded her eyes. 'So that's what
was behind the stone wall. It's absolutely vast. Who
does it belong to?'

'The head of the Ximenes Corporation.' His tone was
indifferent. 'You've heard of that?'

'I think so.' Cressy wrinkled her nose. 'They're in
shipping, aren't they?'

'And banking, and a hotel chain. The founder of the
dynasty was called Alexandros. Like his namesake, he

wished to conquer the world before he was thirty.'
Draco put his hand over hers to alter the tiller. 'Do not
go too close, *agapi mou*.'

'Because intruders aren't welcome?' Cressy pulled a
face. 'Poor rich man.'

'You despise money?' His sideways glance was curious.

'On the contrary. I work long hours to earn as much
as I can.'

'And that is important to you?'

'Well—naturally.'

'More important than being a woman, perhaps?'

Cressy bit her lip, sudden bewilderment battling with
hurt. 'That's a cruel thing to say.'

Draco shrugged a shoulder. 'You are not a child,' he
said. 'You live in a society where sexual freedom is
accepted, and yet you are still a virgin. Why?'

She removed her hand from beneath his. 'I don't
think it's any of your concern.'

'We said we would learn about each other,' he said.
'Yet you refuse to answer a simple question. One that
would solve the mystery about you. Why won't you
explain?'

'You dare say that to me?' She was angry now.
'You're the one with the secrets. You tell me nothing
about yourself.'

'You don't ask.'

'All right.' She drew a deep breath. 'Are your parents
alive?'

'No,' he said. 'But I have aunts and uncles and a
great many cousins. Now, answer my question.'

Cressy hesitated. 'Perhaps I'm out of touch with today's morality,' she said. 'Or maybe I just haven't met
the right man.'

'Ah,' he said softly. 'This great love of which every woman dreams. So, you believe in that.'

I never did before.

Her need for him, her longing, was an aching wound which only he could heal. And it was impossible for him not to know that. So why did he torment her by holding back?

She kept her voice light. 'We're all entitled to our dreams.'

'So, what do you dream of, Cressida *mou*?'

'Oh, dreams are like wishes.' She twisted round, pretending to take a last look at the villa on the headland. 'If you talk about them, they don't come true.'

'Then tell me this,' he said. 'Why did you come back here?'

Cressy swallowed. 'I—I wanted to see more of Myros.'

He sighed impatiently. 'Must I look into your eyes to know the truth, *agapi mou*?'

She said, almost inaudibly, 'And because you asked me…'

'Even though you knew that I wanted you—what I would ask?'

She swung back, tears stinging her eyes. 'Yes,' she said. 'Is that what you want to hear, Kyrios Draco? That I wanted you so much I came back to offer myself…' The stumbling words choked into silence.

'Yes,' he said quietly. 'I—needed to hear that, *agapi mou*.'

His arm encircled her, drawing her against him. 'Don't cry, my golden one—my treasure,' he whispered against her hair as she buried her face in his shoulder. 'And don't be ashamed of what you feel.'

'How can I help it?' Her voice was muffled.

'You imagine I do not want you—because I have been patient?' His voice sank to a whisper. 'I have had to force myself to remain cool, but no longer. I have to speak—to tell you everything in my heart.'

He paused. 'My life is yours, Cressida *mou*. Be my wife and stay with me for ever. Work beside me each day and lie in my arms at night.'

His body was shaking against hers. As she lifted her head she saw the proud face strangely anxious, the firm mouth incredibly vulnerable.

She put up her hand and touched his cheek, brushing her thumb softly across his lips.

She whispered, 'I'll stay...'

He kissed her once, his mouth hard, almost fierce on hers. Telling her beyond doubt how precarious that taut control really was.

'I must wait for more,' he told her as he reluctantly released her, his mouth twisting. 'I want to live with you, my bride, not drown with you.'

She laughed, leaning back in his embrace, the breeze from the sea lifting her hair, happiness warming her like her own private sun.

Lips touching her hair, Draco whispered words of love and need, his voice raw as he switched to his own language.

'I wish I could understand what you're saying,' Cressy sighed, her fingers lightly caressing the strong arm that held her so securely.

'I will tell you one day.' There was a smile in his voice. 'But only when we are married.'

In the hour it took to return to Myros harbour, they also made some practical plans.

It was agreed that Cressy would catch the midday ferry to Alakos, to pack the rest of her things and check out of the Hellenic Imperial. And make a few necessary phone calls, she thought, with a sudden bump of nervousness.

'I would take you myself,' Draco said, frowning. 'But there are things I must do at my house, arrangements I must make.' He paused. 'You'll stay there with me until our marriage, *pethi mou*? You'll trust me?'

'Is that really necessary?' Flushing slightly, Cressy met his gaze directly. 'Draco—I love you. I want to belong to you.'

'And so you will,' he said gently. 'In our house, in our bed, on our wedding night. That is how it must be, Cressida *mou*.'

She shook her head. 'You have a will of iron, *kyrie*.'

His gaze caressed her. 'When you look at me like that, *kyria*, I have no will at all.'

At the taverna, she went up to collect her things, leaving Draco to talk to Yannis.

As she fastened her travel bag she heard a sound behind her, and looked round to find Maria standing in the doorway

'Maria.' Cressy smiled at her a little shyly. 'You've heard the news? I'm hoping very much that you'll lend me your wedding dress again.'

'Kyria Cressida.' Maria took a step forward, her face troubled. 'Are you sure about this? Kyrios Draco—how well do you know him?'

'I know that I love him.'

'You should take care,' Maria said quietly. 'This is not a marriage of equals.'

Cressy bit her lips. 'I understand what you're trying to say. That we'll have to make more adjustments than other couples. But...'

Maria gestured impatiently. 'That is not what I mean. There are things you do not know.'

Cressy stared at her. 'What sort of things?'

Yannis shouted Maria's name from below and she turned to go. 'I cannot say more. But you must be careful.' She left Cressy staring after her.

She was quiet as she walked down to the ferry with Draco at her side.

'Already regrets?' He smiled at her.

'No,' she denied, a little too quickly. She wanted to ask about Maria's warning, but it needed an oblique approach, and there wasn't time because people were already boarding the ferry.

He kissed her mouth, and she felt his thumb trace the sign of the cross on her forehead.

'Come to me soon,' he whispered. 'I shall be waiting for you, my beloved.'

As she collected her key from Hotel Reception, Cressy wondered what the deferential concierge would say if he knew she was planning to marry one of his countrymen.

She'd had time to think on the ferry trip, but hadn't come to any firm conclusions.

Perhaps Maria simply doubted that Draco had sufficient means to support a wife. After all, Cressy had little real idea of what he did for a living, she realised with a touch of unease.

Or had there been something more cynical in her warning? Did Maria suspect that Cressy's real attraction for Draco was as an affluent tourist?

But I'm not rich, and he knows it, Cressy thought. I'm well paid, but when I stop working that'll be it.

And I've still got rent to pay, and bills to settle back in England.

On the other hand even quite modest savings might seem a fortune to an impecunious fisherman.

She found herself remembering the silences—all the times she hadn't known what he was thinking. And, in spite of herself, began to wonder.

That total certainty about the future—her inner radiance—had taken a jolt, but a few doubts were perfectly natural, surely.

Anyway, she and Draco couldn't get married immediately, she reminded herself. There were all kinds of legal and religious formalities to be completed first.

And plenty of time for any lingering qualms to be assuaged.

She was halfway through her packing when the telephone rang.

'Cressy, my dear.'

'Why, Uncle Bob.' She sat down on the edge of the bed. 'What a surprise. I—I was actually planning to call you—'

'Cressy,' he interrupted firmly, 'I'm afraid you must listen carefully. I've got bad news.'

Ten minutes later she replaced the receiver. Her face was colourless and she felt deathly cold.

Her wonderful golden dream had gone, to be replaced by bleak and frightening reality. A chilling reminder of exactly who she was. Not some silly, lovesick child swept away by a handsome face, but a woman with a career, duties and obligations. A woman with a life far removed from some half-finished shack on a piece of Mediterranean rock.

Her father was not only ruined, but alone and ill. He might even be dying. Their recent estrangement was suddenly meaningless. She had to go back to England at once.

For a moment Draco's face seemed to swim in front of her. Gasping, she wrapped her arms round her body. She couldn't let herself think about him, or the folly of the last ten days. She had quite deliberately to wipe him from her mind, and her memory. There was no place for him in her life now, and never had been outside a crazy dream. He was a luxury she couldn't afford, she thought, biting her lip until she tasted blood.

As it was, no real harm had been done, and she had to be thankful for that.

It made her wince to think how naive she'd been—how easily she'd been beguiled to near disaster.

Draco had been so clever, using his sexuality to keep her in a torment of frustration and longing. All those kisses, she thought bitterly. The fleeting caresses that had aroused without satisfying.

And all leading to what? Not marriage, she was certain. He was probably bluffing about that. No, he was counting on her walking away once he'd shown her the life she could expect. But not until she'd handed over a hefty payment for his injured feelings, no doubt.

It was fate, she told herself as the plane took off from Athens. Fate intervening to stop her making the most hideous mistake of her life.

She had to see it like that or she'd go mad. She had to block the pain or she'd moan aloud. Had to tell herself that Draco was just a beach boy on the make or she'd mourn him for ever.

And she had her father's problems to sort out. She had no time for her own.

All very reasoned, Cressy thought now, as she brought her car to a halt in front of the house. Very rational. If only there hadn't been an unknown factor in her equation. A factor that still seemed to be pursuing her.

Cressy spent most of the afternoon on the telephone and sending e-mails, informing her father's creditors that she'd be negotiating on his behalf during his stay in hospital. But if she'd hoped for instant response or co-operation, she was disappointed.

She was just reluctantly deciding to call it a day when she heard the sound of a car outside and her uncle appeared, accompanied by Charles Lawrence, her father's legal adviser.

Sir Robert spoke without preamble. 'Cressy—have you spoken to the bank?'

She shook her head. 'They put me off with polite noises. Why—have you heard something?'

'I was contacted this morning.' Charles Lawrence was speaking. 'It's an extraordinary business, Cressida. They've had an offer to pay off the mortgage on this house, and your father's other debts. Someone's prepared to—take them over.'

'Just like that?' Cressy stared at both men. 'But that's impossible.'

Mr Lawrence nodded. 'So I thought. But I've since spoken to the other party, and the offer has been confirmed.'

Cressy mentally reviewed her father's close friends. There were several millionaires among them, but she wouldn't have credited any of them with that level of generosity.

She said doubtfully, 'Is it Dad's old company—have they put together a rescue package for him?'

'Nothing like that, I fear. The offer has come from

the Standard Trust Bank. They are based in New York, but they're owned by the Ximenes Corporation. I expect you've heard of it.'

'Yes.' Her voice sounded odd, suddenly, almost distorted. 'Yes—it was mentioned to me quite recently.'

'Well, I don't understand any of it,' Sir Robert said bluntly. 'Who are these people, and what on earth have they to do with James? I wasn't aware he'd had any dealings with them.'

'I'm sure he didn't.' Charles Lawrence shook his head. 'It's a complete mystery, but I hope Cressida may be able to solve it.' He gave her a bleak smile. 'It seems they wish to negotiate with you personally, my dear.'

'Did they give any particular reason?' Cressy felt hollow as weird, incredible suspicions continued to ferment in her mind.

No, she thought. It's not true. It can't be. It's just an odd coincidence. It has to be—*has to*...

'No, but I got the impression that the chairman—a chap called Viannis—is a law unto himself.' He consulted some notes. 'He's staying in London at the Grand Imperial—occupies the penthouse, apparently. You're to phone for an appointment.'

'Well, I don't like the sound of it,' Sir Robert said restively. 'You're James's solicitor. He should be talking to you.'

'I suggested as much, but they were adamant. It has to be Cressida. Although she can always refuse,' he added quickly.

'No,' Cressy said. 'If this Viannis is prepared to throw my father a lifeline, then I'll talk to him, or anyone. I'll call tomorrow and fix up a meeting.'

'Well,' Sir Robert said dubiously, 'if you're quite sure, my dear.'

After their departure Cressy sat for a while, staring into space. Then she rose and went over to the desk and her laptop.

The e-mail icon was waiting for her, as she'd suspected it would be.

Swallowing, she clicked on to the message.

'Sid,' she read. 'I am waiting for you. Come to me.'

And that meant there could no longer be any doubt at all.

'Oh, God,' she whispered, her clenched fist pressed against her mouth. 'What am I going to do?'

CHAPTER SEVEN

As THE gates closed and the lift began its smooth rush to the penthouse, Cressy drew a deep breath.

Whatever—whoever—was waiting for her, it was essential that she appear composed and in control. She couldn't afford to let the mask slip for a moment and reveal the turmoil of emotion inside her.

She had dressed carefully for this meeting. Her navy blue suit was immaculate, the skirt cut decorously to the knee. The heavy cream silk blouse buttoned to the throat, and she wore neat navy pumps with a medium heel and carried a briefcase. Her hair had been brushed severely back from her face and confined at the nape of her neck with a gilt clip.

Her make-up had been meticulously applied to cover up the tell-tale signs of another sleepless night.

She looked, she thought, cool and businesslike. She hoped she was going to be treated accordingly.

She thought, not for the first time, her throat tightening uncontrollably, Oh, let him be a stranger. Please—*please* let me be wrong about this...

She was met on the top floor by a tall blonde man with a transatlantic accent, who greeted her unsmilingly and introduced himself as Paul Nixon, Mr Viannis's personal assistant.

He led her down the thickly carpeted corridor and knocked at the double doors at the end.

He said, 'Miss Fielding is here, sir,' and stood aside to allow Cressy to go in.

The room was full of light. There were huge windows on three sides, permitting panoramic views all over London.

But Cressy was only aware of the tall, dark figure silhouetted against the brightness. For a moment she was scarcely able to breathe, and she halted abruptly, feeling as if a giant fist had clenched in her stomach, all her worst fears finally and inevitably confirmed.

He was very still, but with the tension of a coiled spring. Across the room, his anger reached out and touched her, and she had to fight an impulse to flinch. Or even run...

He said softly, 'So, you have come to me at last— Cressida, my faithless one.'

There was a note in his voice which sent a shiver between her shoulder blades, but it was vital not to seem afraid.

She lifted her chin. 'Mr Viannis?'

'What charming formality.' The mockery in his tone was savage. 'You feel it's appropriate—under the circumstances? After all, how do you address your ex-fiancé—someone you've so signally betrayed?'

She said steadily, 'I came here to negotiate a deal for my father, not indulge in useless recriminations.'

'No,' he said. 'You came here to accept my terms. There is nothing to negotiate.'

She'd hoped to find a stranger and in some ways her wish had been granted, because this wasn't Draco. This man had never worn scruffy denims or danced in the sunlight. Had never kissed her, or smiled at her with lazy desire. Could never, even for a few breathless moments, have held her naked in his arms.

This man looked thinner—older, she thought, her eyes scanning him with sudden bewilderment. His charcoal suit with its faint pinstripe was exquisitely cut, his tie a paler grey silk.

The tumbled black hair had been tamed and trimmed. And there was no golden light in the dark eyes that met hers. They were cold—impenetrable.

Even his voice was different. Now he spoke with hardly any accent at all.

She thought, How could I not have seen it—the ruthlessness behind the golden sunlit charm?

He walked over to the big desk in the centre of the room and sat down, curtly indicating that she should occupy the chair set at the opposite side.

She obeyed reluctantly. Her legs were shaking and her heart was thudding unevenly.

She said, struggling to keep her voice level, 'How did you find me?'

'You were staying in one of my hotels, so that provided the basic information.' He shrugged. 'After that, I had enquiries made.'

'You checked up on me?' Her voice was taut. 'Was this before or after you asked me to marry you?'

His smile did not reach his eyes. 'Oh, long before. When we first encountered each other. I needed to be sure that you were just as you seemed.'

'I'm glad I measured up to your exacting requirements.' She spoke with deliberate disdain, trying to cover her growing unease.

'That was then,' he said. 'This is now.'

Cressy touched the tip of her tongue to her dry lips, realising too late that Draco had seen and marked that tiny act of self-betrayal.

She hurried into speech. 'And that's how you discovered my father's—difficulties, I suppose?'

'Yes,' he said. 'But they are hardly "difficulties". Your father is facing total ruin.'

'I know that,' she said. 'Which is the reason I'm here today.'

'No,' he said. 'You are here because you ran away. Because you left me without a word. You are here to explain.'

'My father collapsed,' she said flatly. 'He was in Intensive Care. I—had to come back.'

'Without one word to the man you had just promised to marry?' His voice bit.

Cressy's hands were clenched so tightly in her lap that her fingers ached. She said, 'I didn't think that either of us took that seriously. A lot of women have— flings on foreign holidays.'

'Ah.' Draco leaned back in the tall leather chair. 'So you saw our relationship as some trivial, transient affair. A thing of no consequence.' His tone suggested courteous interest, but she wasn't fooled.

'In some ways,' she said uncertainly.

He said slowly, 'If that was true, I would have taken you on the beach that first afternoon and you would have spent the rest of your holiday in my bed.'

'And eventually gone on my way with a diamond necklace, I suppose,' Cressy flashed.

'Perhaps.' He sounded indifferent. 'If you'd pleased me sufficiently.'

'I can't think why you held back.'

'Because I was fool enough to respect your innocence, Cressida *mou*.' His tone was harsh. 'I did not see it was just a physical attribute. That, in reality, you were just as calculating and heartless as your namesake.'

Cressy leaned forward. 'You think I've treated you badly,' she said hotly. 'But you weren't honest with me either. You deliberately let me think you were poor. Why?'

'An unaccountable need to be wanted for myself only, and not for my worldly goods,' he drawled. 'It was so refreshing to meet someone who had no idea who I was, *pethi mou*.'

'And how long did you plan to go on deceiving me?' She realised now why Maria had tried to warn her. To tell her that she was involved with a man who was not only very rich, but powerful. A man who would live up to his name if crossed.

'It would have been over as soon as you returned from Alakos. You see, *agapi mou*, I had planned a big party for our engagement at my house.'

She stared at him. 'It belongs to you, doesn't it? That wonderful villa on the headland?'

'Yes,' he said. 'My family and friends were flying in from all over the world to meet you—my future wife— there.'

'Oh.' Cressy felt sick.

'At first I thought you had simply missed the ferry,' he went on, as if she hadn't spoken. 'I called the hotel, and they told me you had checked out, so I waited for a message. I waited a long time. I cannot remember the precise moment I realised you were not coming back.'

'My father needed me,' she said desperately. 'I had to get to Athens—to go to him.'

'And it never occurred to you to turn to me—the man you'd professed to love?' His mouth twisted contemptuously. 'What a mistake, Cressida *mou*. My helicopter would have flown us to Athens. My private plane would have taken us on to London. You would have been there in half the time.'

'But I had no means of knowing that,' she protested.

'If you had come to me you would have known. Only you didn't. And that is the worst thing of all. To know that you were in trouble—in pain—yet you didn't want to share this with me. Even if I'd been as poor as you thought, at least I had the right to put my arms around you and hold you.

'As it was, I could have taken you straight to your father and been with you to comfort and care for you, as a man should with his woman.' He paused, the dark eyes merciless. 'Tell me, *pethi mou*, had you any intention of contacting me again—ever? Or was I simply to be—erased, like an unfortunate mistake in a calculation?'

Cressy shook her head, feeling tears thickening in her throat. 'Draco—I don't know—I was worried—confused...'

'Then let me tell you the answer,' he said. 'You didn't love—and you didn't trust either. That was the bitter truth I had to learn. I was poor, so I could be discarded, as if I had no feelings. And one day you will discover how that feels. Because I shall teach you.'

He smiled at her. 'You will discover, Cressida *mou*, that I am not so easily forgotten.'

She said in a low voice, 'I suppose you mean to use my father's problems against me. Well—I'm prepared for that.'

'Are you?' he asked softly. 'I had originally intended to present the settlement of his debts as a gift to you when we announced our engagement. Since then I have had time to think again.'

She said urgently, 'Draco—whatever you think of me—please don't punish my father any more. He's a sick man.'

'And when he leaves hospital he will need a home

to go to,' he said. 'The house that now belongs to me. Is that what you're trying to put into words?'

She said on a note of desperation, 'I could pay rent...'

'Yes, you will pay,' he said quietly. 'But not with money. I have enough of that already.'

'Then how?' Her voice was barely more than a whisper.

'Don't you know?' he said. 'Don't you understand that I still want you?'

The room was very still suddenly. She stared across the desk at him. At the hard bronze face and the cool mouth that looked as if it would never smile again. Watched and waited for some softening—some warmth. But in vain.

She swallowed. 'You mean—in spite of everything— you're going to marry me?'

His laugh was harsh. 'No, not marriage, my sweet. I will not be caught again. This time I'm offering a less formal arrangement.' He added cynically, 'And spare me the pretence that you don't understand my offer.'

'I understand.' Her voice seemed to come from a long way away. 'You're saying that if I—sleep with you— you won't enforce the mortgage or my father's other debts.'

'Yes,' he said softly. 'I am saying exactly that. And what is your answer?'

She said hoarsely, 'Draco, you can't mean this. If you loved me, you wouldn't...'

'I said that I wanted you, Cressida *mou*. I did not mention love.'

Pain ripped at her, tearing her apart. She hadn't realised it was possible to hurt so much. Or to be so afraid.

She said, her voice shaking, 'Is this your idea of revenge? To rape me?'

'No,' he said. 'Because you will come to me willingly, Cressida, as we both know.'

'Never.'

He shrugged. 'Then regard it simply as a business transaction. You understand those better than you know yourself, I think.'

'Business?' Her voice cracked. 'How can it be that?'

'I have something you want.' His smile mocked her. 'You have something I want. That's how deals are made.'

'You make it sound so simple.'

'It is hardly complicated.' His voice was cool, and oddly impersonal. 'You will come to me, and stay with me as long as I require. When our liaison ends, I will hand over the mortgage and other papers—instead of a diamond necklace,' he added, his mouth twisting.

'And if I refuse this—degrading offer?'

He leaned back in his chair. He said quietly, 'We have already established that your father's well-being is your sole priority. So I do not think we need consider that possibility—do you?'

'No.' Her voice was barely audible. 'No, I don't—really—have a choice.'

He smiled thinly. 'You've made the right decision.' He got to his feet and came round the desk to her side. He took her hand, pulling her out of the chair.

He led her across the room to a door, which he opened, revealing a large and luxurious bedroom.

'You mean—now?' Her voice rose, and she recoiled, swinging round to face him. 'Oh, God, you can't be serious.'

His brows lifted. 'Why not?'

She said wildly, 'Because it's the middle of the morning.'

He began to laugh. 'How conventional you are, *agapi mou*,' he mocked. 'When we were on Myros there was not one minute of the day or night that we did not want each other.'

She bit her lip. 'That was different.'

'Did you expect me to seduce you over dinner with flowers and moonlight?' His tone was cynical. 'It is too late for that. Once, perhaps, I would have made it beautiful for you. Now—' he shrugged '—regard it as the signature on a contract.'

'Draco.' Her voice broke. 'Please—don't do this to me—to us.'

'Us?' he echoed contemptuously. 'There is no "us". I have bought you, Cressida *mou*. That is all. And this time you will not have the opportunity to run away.' He glanced at his watch. 'I have a couple of calls to make. I will join you in a few minutes.'

She said bitterly, 'You're enjoying this, aren't you?'

'I intend to,' he said. 'Whether or not you share my pleasure is your own concern. But I think you will.'

He pulled her towards him, his arm a steel band forcing her compliance. His dark face swam momentarily in front of her startled eyes. Then he bent his head and kissed her breast.

The sudden heat of his mouth scorched through her thin blouse and lacy bra as if she was already naked. His lips found her nipple, tugging at it, creating a sharp, exquisite pain that triggered a scalding flood of need in return.

Surprised and shamed at the physical fierceness of her response, Cressy gasped, her hands curling into impotent fists at her sides.

When he lifted his head he was smiling faintly. He reached for one small clenched hand and raised it to his lips with insolent grace.

His other hand slid down over her hip to her thigh, and lingered there suggestively.

He said softly, 'Nothing has really changed between us, Cressida *mou*. Only the terms of our coming together. Shall I prove it to you? Show you exactly how much you still want me?'

Helpless colour warmed her face. She shook her head, staring down at the carpet, not daring to meet the intensity of his gaze. Scared of what else she might betray.

She had not bargained for the overwhelming force of instinct. But that could be harnessed, she told herself. Hidden.

For her own sake, she had to try.

She found herself impelled gently but inexorably into the bedroom. She began a last protest, but Draco laid a finger on her parted lips, silencing her.

He said, 'I shall try not to keep you waiting too long.'

The door closed behind him, shutting her in. She stood, her arms wrapped defensively across her body, staring round.

It was a big room, and the bed was its dominant feature, wide and low, with a dark green cover tailored in heavy linen, matching the drapes at the windows.

A very masculine room, she thought, comfortable but impersonal. A suitable place for a bargain, but not for love. Never for love.

She walked across and tugged at the cords, swinging the curtains across to block out the brilliant sunlight. She wanted shadows, she thought. Shadows and darkness to hide in.

She needed, too, to blot out the searing memory of those other golden days on Myros when she had turned to him, eagerly offering her mouth—her body.

Her whole body seemed to stir in sudden yearning, and regret, and she stiffened, bringing her rebellious senses back under control once more. She could not allow herself such weakness.

Whatever Draco did to her—no matter how he made her feel—somehow she had to stay aloof—and endure.

Presently, she thought, I shall wake up and find all this was just a nightmare.

She looked back, dry-mouthed, at the bed, pain searing through her as she realised how different it could have been.

But she'd made her choice—a whole series of choices—and she had to live with the consequences. Starting now...

She left her clothes in the adjoining dressing room. The carpet was soft under her bare feet as she walked to the bed. The percale sheets felt crisp and cool against her burning skin as she lay tensely, waiting for the door to open.

Which, eventually, just as her nerves had reached screaming point, it did.

'Shy, *agapi mou*?' He was a dark shape at the end of the bed. He turned away, walking over to the windows and flinging back the drapes again, flooding the room with sudden light.

Draco came back to the bed. For a moment he stood staring down at her, then he reached down, twitching the covers from her outraged fingers and tossing them to the foot of the bed.

He said softly, 'A man likes to look, as well as touch.'

Teeth set defiantly, Cressy withstood his lingering scrutiny, deliberately not covering herself with her hands, nor looking away, even when he began, almost casually, to remove his clothes.

Only when he came to lie beside her on the bed and drew her into his arms did she finally close her eyes, her body rigid against his naked warmth.

The scent of his skin, once so familiar and so precious, now admixed with a trace of some expensive cologne, pervaded her mouth and nose, so that she seemed to be breathing him, absorbing him into every atom of her consciousness.

She remembered one day on the beach, kissing his shoulder, tasting the heat of the sun and the salt of the sea on its curving muscularity. But she couldn't afford those kind of memories. She had to lie still and unyielding—and hate. Resentment would be her only salvation.

But it wasn't easy, not when his hands had begun to caress her, the warm fingers skimming over her flesh in exquisite, tantalising exploration.

As they softly brushed her taut nipples Cressy had to bite back a gasp, her body clenching in hot, shamed excitement.

Where his hands touched, his mouth followed. He kissed her breasts softly, his tongue unhurriedly circling each puckered rose peak in turn. Sensation, knife-sharp and honey-sweet, pierced through her, making her quiver and arch towards him involuntarily, and she felt his lips smile against her skin.

His hand parted her thighs and began to stroke her, delicately, subtly, making her moan and writhe against the intimate play of his fingers as they promised—tantalised—and then denied.

Every sense, every atom of consciousness was focused painfully on that tiny, pulsating centre of her being as she felt herself being drawn slowly and exquisitely to some undreamed of brink. As she felt her breath quicken and heard the frantic drumming of her own heart.

She made a small, wounded sound in her throat. A wordless plea for him—somehow—to end this beautiful torment.

'Not yet.' His tongue caressed the whorls of her ear. 'Not yet, but—soon...' And his hand moved fractionally, deepening the caress. Imposing a more compelling demand.

She was blind, deaf—mindless. Aware of nothing but the fierce concentration of pleasure that he was creating for her. As if the sun, beating against her eyelids, was blooming and growing inside her.

And when, at last, he gave her the release she craved, she cried out in harsh animal delight as ripple upon ripple of pure feeling engulfed her—convulsed her. As she was flung out into space, where she fell into the centre of the sun and was consumed.

She was totally relaxed, her body still throbbing with pleasure, as Draco moved above her, and, with one deep thrust, into her.

For a fleeting instant she was scared by the memory of pain, then shocked by its absence. Because now there was only joyous acceptance, and a sense of completion.

As if, she thought, this was the moment she had been made for.

She raised her languid lids and stared up at him, letting herself enclose him. Hold him.

Allowing herself to savour how alien it felt, yet at the same time how totally familiar—and precious.

The bronze face was stark, his eyes like pits of darkness as he began to move, slowly and powerfully, inside her.

Instinct lifted her hands to his shoulders and clasped her legs round his lean hips, so that she could partner him completely. Could mirror each compelling stroke.

As the rhythm and intensity increased, Draco groaned something in his own language. She kissed his throat, licking the salt from his skin, feeling the thunder of his pulse against her lips.

At the same time, deep within her, she was aware of the first flutterings of renewed delight. Incredulous, gasping, she held him closer, her sweat mingling with his as the spiral of pleasure tautened unbearably, then imploded.

Her whole body rocked as the tremors of rapture tore through her, echoed by the wild spasms of his own climax.

When it was over, he lay very still, his face against her breasts.

She wanted to hold him. To put her lips against the damp, dark tangle of hair and whisper that she loved him. That as he'd been the first, so would he be the last.

As his cherished bride, it would have been her right to open her heart to him. As his mistress—she sank her teeth into her swollen lower lip—she had no rights at all. And that was something she must never forget. That her role in his life was at best transient.

At last he stirred, lifting himself away from her. He reached for his watch from the night table, grimaced at the time, and fastened the thin gold bracelet back on his wrist. Then he turned and looked down at Cressy, his dark eyes almost dispassionate.

'Thank you.' His voice was cool, even faintly

amused. 'I had not expected such—enchanting co-operation. You learn quickly.'

'Is—is that all you have to say?' Her voice shook. She felt as if she'd been slapped.

'No, but the rest must wait. I have a meeting in the City. But you don't have to leave,' he added swiftly as Cressy half sat up. 'No one will disturb you if you wish to sleep.'

'I don't,' she said curtly. 'I haven't visited my father today. I need to get back there.'

He nodded, unfazed. 'Paul will contact you with your instructions.'

'Instructions?'

'I shall soon be returning to Greece. I require you to accompany me.'

'But my job—my father,' Cressy protested. 'I can't just—go.'

'You will find that you can. Your employer has been most understanding. Your—services are on temporary loan to me. I did not explain the exact nature of the services,' he added with a shrug. 'So you can tell him as much or as little as you wish.'

She swallowed. 'My God,' she said. 'You don't allow much to stand in your way, do you? Suppose I'd turned you down.'

'I was certain you wouldn't.' His mouth twisted. 'Apart from other considerations, your sexual curiosity had been aroused, *agapi mou*, and needed to be satisfied.' His hand touched her shoulder, then travelled swiftly and sensuously down her body. It was the lightest of caresses but it brought her skin stinglingly alive.

Draco's laugh was soft. 'You see, Cressida *mou*, even now you are eager for your next lesson. How sad that I have not more time to devote to you.'

Cressy reached down and dragged the discarded sheet up over her body. She recognised that it was basically a meaningless gesture, but it made her feel marginally better.

She forced herself to meet his gaze. She said, 'You mentioned I was on loan to you. For how long, exactly?'

Draco swung his long legs to the floor. 'I said three months initially.'

She said, 'I—see.'

The blissful euphoria which had followed their love-making had gone. In its place, pain and shame were dragging her apart.

'I suggest you see a doctor as a matter of urgency,' he tossed over his shoulder as he walked to the bathroom. 'Today I used protection, but even so we must ensure there's no chance of you becoming pregnant.'

Cressy was suddenly very still, her eyes enormous as she stared after him.

With a few casual words, she thought, he'd relegated her to the status of a non-person.

Yet this was the reality of the situation. She was no longer his golden love. She was a temporary sexual partner. And the skill and artistry he'd brought to her initiation had simply been a means to an end. Draco had ensured her pleasure merely to increase his own.

And if she'd hoped in some secret corner of her mind that the glory of their coming together would soften his attitude towards her, she knew better now, and disappointment twisted inside her like a claw.

There were tears crowding in her throat, stinging the backs of her eyes, but she would not shed them in front of him.

She said quietly. 'No—of course not.'

The bathroom door closed behind him, and presently she heard the sound of the shower running.

She released a trembling breath. Somehow she had to come to terms with the relationship that he'd offered her, and all its limitations, when the most she could hope for was that it would soon be over.

'Oh, God,' she whispered brokenly. 'How can I bear it?'

And she turned her face into the pillow and lay like a stone.

CHAPTER EIGHT

SHE pretended to be asleep when Draco came back into the bedroom, lying motionless, her eyes tightly shut, as she listened with nerves jangling to his quiet movements, the rustle of clothing as he dressed.

When, at last, he came across to the bed, she forced her tense body into deep relaxation, keeping her breathing soft and even.

She thought she heard him sigh as he turned away, but she couldn't be sure.

It was some time after she heard the bedroom door click shut behind him that she ventured to sit up, and make sure she was really alone.

She thought, I have to get out of here. I don't want anyone to see me—to know...

She knew she was being ridiculous. That there wasn't a member of Draco's staff who wouldn't be perfectly aware of the situation. She just didn't want to find herself face to face with any of them.

She was scared, too, that if she gave way to sleep she might still be here when Draco returned.

She showered swiftly, but if she hoped to wash away the touch and taste of him it was in vain. His possession had been total. He was irrevocably part of her now, and there was nothing she could do about it.

She shivered as she towelled her damp hair.

What had happened to all her high-flown plans about fighting him—about remaining indifferent? she wondered bitterly.

One kiss—his hand on her breast—and all her resolution had crumbled. Indeed, she could hardly have made it easier for him. She wanted to hate him for the way he had made her feel, but she hated herself more.

There were mirrors all round the bathroom, throwing back images of a girl whose eyes were heavy with newly learned secrets. The cool lady she'd been so proud of had vanished for ever, swept away on a frantic tide of passion.

Yet the encounter had left no visible marks on her skin, she thought, with detached surprise. Her mouth was reddened and slightly swollen, and she ached a little, but that was all.

I got off lightly, she told herself. But she knew in her heart that it wasn't true.

When she was dressed, she looked at herself and winced. All those carefully chosen garments—the business suit and prim shirt—had been worn as armour, yet they'd proved no protection at all.

She went back to her flat and changed into a plain black shift, sleeveless and severe, stuffing the discarded clothing into a refuse sack. She never wanted to see any of it again. She thrust her bare feet into sandals and grabbed a simple cream linen jacket before going down to her car.

It was a nightmare journey, a battle between her need to concentrate on the road and the storm of bewildered emotion within her. But at last she reached the hospital.

In one piece, but only just, she thought grimly.

As she waited for the lift to take her up to the ICU, she was waylaid by a nurse.

'Your father's been moved, Miss Fielding. He's made such good progress over the last twenty-four hours that he's in a private room on ''A'' wing now.'

'You mean he's getting better? But that's wonderful.' Cressy's mouth trembled into a relieved smile. 'Because he looked so ill when I was here last.'

'Oh, he's still being carefully monitored, but everyone's very pleased with him.' The older woman beamed. 'Mind you, I think all the goodies he's been receiving—the fruit and flowers from Mrs Fielding—have cheered him up a lot.'

'Eloise has sent fruit and flowers?' Cressy repeated incredulously.

'Well, there wasn't an actual card, but he said they must be from her. He was so thrilled.' She paused. 'Is Mrs Fielding not with you today? What a shame.'

When she reached her father's room, it looked like a florist's window.

As she paused in the doorway, admiring the banks of blooms, James Fielding turned an eager head towards her, his welcoming smile fading when he saw who it was.

'Cressy, my dear.' He spoke with an effort, failing to mask the disappointment in his voice. 'How good to see you.'

'You look marvellous, Daddy.' She went to the bed and kissed his cheek. 'I've never seen so many flowers. I'd have brought some, but they didn't allow them in ICU, and now everyone else has beaten me to it.' She was aware she was chattering, trying to cover up the awkward moment. Attempting to hide the instinctive hurt provoked by his reaction.

He didn't want it to be me, she thought with desolation. He hoped it was Eloise. That she'd come back to him.

'Those lilies and carnations over there, and the fruit basket, came without a card,' her father said eagerly.

'But I think I know who they're from.' He smiled tenderly. 'In fact, I'm sure. I just wish she'd signed her name. But perhaps she felt diffident about that—under the circumstances.'

Diffident? Cressy wanted to scream. Eloise hasn't an insecure bone in her body.

Instead, she forced a smile as she sat down beside his bed. 'Yes—perhaps...'

He played with the edge of the sheet, frowning a little. 'Has she been in contact—left any message at all?'

Cressy shook her head. 'There's been nothing. Daddy. Don't you think I'd have told you?'

'I don't know,' he said with a touch of impatience. 'Certainly there's never been any love lost between you.'

'Well, that's unimportant now.' She put a hand over his. 'All that matters is that you get well.'

'The consultant says I can go home soon, if I keep up this progress. But he wants me to have a live-in nurse for a while. He feels it will be too much for Berry.'

His frown deepened. 'I wasn't sure that my insurance covered private nursing, but he says it's all taken care of.' He paused. 'What I need to know is—do I still have a home to go to?'

She said gently, 'Yes, you have, darling. I've managed to do a deal with your creditors. You can go on living at the house.'

He nodded. 'That's good. I'd have hated Eloise to find the place all shut up, or occupied by strangers, and not know where to find me. Because it won't last—this Alec Caravas thing. She's had her head turned by a younger man, that's all.'

Cressy's lips parted in a silent gasp of incredulity.

For a moment she could feel the blood drumming in her ears and felt physically sick.

Was that really his only concern—providing a bolt-hole for his worthless wife—if she chose to return? Didn't he realise she'd been Alec Caravas's full accomplice—and that the police would want to interview her if she ever dared show her face again?

She'd expected her father to ask all sorts of awkward questions about the exact accommodation she'd reached over his debts, but he didn't seem remotely interested. Instead he just took it for granted that she'd managed to get things sorted.

Just as he'd tacitly accepted the estrangement between them that Eloise had imposed, she realised with a sudden ache of the heart.

And he would never have any conception of the terrible personal price she'd been forced to pay on his behalf.

I've ruined my life to get him out of trouble, Cressy thought with anguish. And he doesn't even care. Nothing matters except this obsession with Eloise.

She got clumsily to her feet. 'I—I'd better go. I promised the nurses I wouldn't tire you.'

'Perhaps it would be best.' He leaned back against his pillows, reaching for the radio headphones.

She took a deep breath. 'But there's something I must tell you first. I—I have to go abroad very soon—to work. It's a special contract. It may take a few months.'

'Well, that's excellent news.' His smile held some of the old warmth. 'I hope it means more money—or a promotion. You deserve it, you know.'

She said quietly, 'I'm not sure what I deserve any more. And I'm not certain if I should go—if I should leave you.'

'Nonsense, darling. Of course you must go. We both have our own lives to lead. We can't be dependent on each other. And the last thing I want is you fussing round me. Berry and this nurse will be bad enough.'

'No,' she said. 'You're probably right. I—I'll see you tomorrow.'

She went quietly to the door and let herself out. In the corridor, she stopped and leaned against the wall, aware that her legs were shaking so badly she thought she might collapse. She closed her eyes as a scalding tear forced its way under her lid and down her cheek.

She thought brokenly, Oh, Daddy...

'Miss Fielding—is something wrong?' A nurse's anxious voice invaded her torturous thoughts.

Cressy straightened quickly. 'No—it's all right.' She tried a little laugh. 'I think the worry of the past few days has just caught up with me, that's all.'

'I'm not surprised. Oh, and talking of surprises...' The girl felt in the pocket of her uniform. 'You know the fruit and flowers that arrived for your father with no name on them? Well, they've just found this card in Reception. It must have fallen off when the delivery was made.' She beamed. 'One mystery solved.' She lowered her voice significantly. 'Although I think he was hoping they were from Mrs Fielding.'

Cressy held out her hand. 'May I look?'

The signature was a slash of black ink across the rectangle of pasteboard. *'Draco Viannis.'*

She wasn't even surprised. She closed her hand on the card, feeling its sharp edges dig into her palm. Wanting it to hurt. Needing a visible scar to counterbalance all the inner pain.

She said quietly, 'Thank you. I'll—see that he gets

it. Now, is it possible for me to have a word with the consultant?'

She didn't go straight back to the house. There was a National Trust property a few miles away, whose grounds were open to the public. There was an Elizabethan knot garden, and a lake with swans, and Cressy had always loved it there.

She found an unoccupied bench and sat, gazing across the sunlit waters with eyes that saw nothing and a heart without peace.

Her father had needed her, she thought, so she'd turned her back on the love that Draco was offering and gone running to him. She'd wanted, just once more, to be the cherished only daughter—to bask in the old relationship. To be important to him again.

But that was always going to be impossible, she realised wearily. Because they were not the same people any longer. Life had moved on for both of them.

So why this last vain attempt to cling on to her childhood?

She looked down at her hands, clenched in her lap. She remembered other hands, dark against her pale skin, and shivered.

She thought, Was I really so afraid of becoming a woman? Was that the true reason I ran away from Draco?

Under the circumstances, her reluctance to face the challenge of her own sexuality was ironic. Because Draco himself had changed all that in one brief, but very succinct lesson.

And now she was left stranded, between his desire for revenge and her father's indifference.

I've wrecked everything, she told herself desolately.

Sacrificed the only chance of real happiness I've ever been offered.

But she couldn't let herself think about that, or she would break down completely. And she had to be strong to get through the next few weeks or months, living on the edge of Draco's life. Strong enough, too, to walk away with her head high when it was over.

And before that she had other problems to deal with.

Her father might be too preoccupied with the loss of his wife to question this 'job abroad' too closely, but her aunt and uncle might not be so incurious. They would want a full explanation, and she couldn't imagine what she would say to them—or to Berry, who would find it unthinkable for her to leave her father in this way.

And how could she explain why her father's debts were now in abeyance, and the house reprieved, without mentioning the precise terms of her 'contract' with Draco?

Her conversation with the consultant had been uncomfortably revealing. Over the years her father's health cover had been reduced to a minimum. The top-grade private room he was occupying, and the services of the live-in nurse, were being paid for by Draco.

'I thought you knew and approved, Miss Fielding,' the consultant had told her, frowning. 'He described himself as a close friend of the family.'

'Yes,' she'd said, dry-mouthed. 'Yes, of course.'

It seemed there was not a part of her life that Draco didn't control. And the fact that in this instance his influence was totally benign somehow made it no better.

Oh, God, she thought. It's all such a mess.

And began, soundlessly and uncontrollably, to cry until she had no more tears left.

It was the sudden chill of the evening breeze across the lake and the clang of the bell announcing that the grounds were closing that eventually roused her from her unhappy reverie.

It was more than time she was getting back. Berry would have dinner waiting for her and would be worried about her non-appearance, she thought, sighing, as she returned reluctantly to her car.

The hall lights were on when she let herself into the house, but there was no sign of the housekeeper—or of dinner either. No place laid in the dining room or welcoming aroma of food in the air. Just—silence.

She called, 'Berry—I'm home,' and waited, but there was no response.

Maybe she'd gone into the garden, to pick some last-minute fruit for dessert or bring in some washing, Cressy thought, subduing an unwelcome tingle of apprehension.

She walked to the drawing room door, twisted the handle, and went in.

Draco was standing beside the fireplace, one arm resting on the mantelshelf as he stared down at the empty grate. He turned slightly, the dark eyes narrowing as Cressy paused in the doorway, her hand going to her throat in shock.

He said softly, 'So here you are at last, *agapi mou*. I have been waiting for you.'

She said shakily, 'So I see. Where's Berry? What's happened to her?'

His brows lifted. 'Naturally, I have murdered her and buried her body under the lawn,' he returned caustically. 'Or so you seem to think.'

She bit her lip. 'I don't think anything of the kind,' she denied curtly, aware that her heart was hammering in a totally unwelcome way at the sight of him. But then he'd startled her—hadn't he?

'I was just a little anxious about her,' she added defensively.

'So many anxieties about so many people.' His smile did not reach his eyes. 'What a caring heart you have, my golden girl. The truth is that I gave your Mrs Berryman the evening off. I believe she means to go to a cinema.'

'You gave Berry the evening off?' She stared at him, open-mouthed. 'And she agreed?'

His mouth twisted. 'She was a little reluctant at first, but I can be very persuasive.'

'To hell with your powers of persuasion,' Cressy lifted her chin. 'You had no right to do anything of the sort.'

'I have all kinds of rights, Cressida *mou*.' His tone hardened. 'And I mean to enjoy all of them.' He held out a hand. 'Now come and welcome me properly.'

Mutinously, she walked forward and stood in front of him. When he kissed her she stood unmoving, unresponding to the warm, sensuous pressure of his lips on hers.

After a moment, he drew back.

'Sulking?' he asked. 'What's the matter? Did I hurt you, perhaps, this morning?'

Colour rushed into her face. She stared down at the carpet. 'I don't know.'

He said, 'Look at me, *matia mou*. Look at me and say that.'

Cressy raised her eyes unwillingly to him. His smile was faintly mocking, but there was an odd watchfulness in his gaze which she found unnerving.

She said, 'No—no, you didn't. As you know quite well.'

'Where you are concerned, my beautiful one, I suspect I know very little.' His tone was dry. 'But I am glad you did not find your first surrender too much of an ordeal.'

She threw her head back defiantly. 'Your words, *kyrie*. Not mine. And now perhaps you'd tell me what you're doing here.'

'I thought I should pay a visit,' he said. 'To make sure that all was well with my property.' He paused. 'But I see it is not.' He took her chin in his hand, studying her, ignoring her gasp of outrage. 'You have been crying, *pethi mou*. Why?'

'Do you really need to ask that?' She freed herself stormily and stepped back. 'Or did you imagine I'd be turning cartwheels for joy because the mighty Draco Viannis had sex with me today.'

His mouth tightened. 'Would you have wept if Draco the fisherman had taken you that day on Myros?'

'He didn't exist,' she said. 'So how can I know?'

'You could always—pretend.'

She shook her head. 'There's been too much pretence already. Now we have a business arrangement.'

'Ah, yes,' he said softly. He removed his jacket, tossed it over the arm of one of the sofas and sat down, loosening his tie.

He smiled at her. 'Then perhaps you would take off your dress—strictly in the line of business.'

Her skin warmed again, hectically. 'My—dress?'

'To begin with.' His tie followed the jacket, and he began, unhurriedly, to unbutton his shirt.

She said, 'You—you actually expect me to strip for you?'

'It is hardly a novelty.' His tone was dry. 'After all, Cressida *mou*, the first time I saw your beautiful breasts it was your own idea.'

Her voice trembled. 'I—hate you.'

He laughed. 'That should add an extra dimension to the way you remove your clothes, my lovely one. I cannot wait.'

She said, 'But someone might come…'

He grinned at her. 'More than one, I hope, *agapi mou*.'

To her fury, she realised she was blushing again. 'You know what I mean.'

'Yes,' he said. 'And why do you think I gave the housekeeper leave of absence? Precisely so we should not be disturbed. Now, will you take off your dress, or do you wish me to do it for you?'

'No.' Her voice was a thread. 'I'll do it.'

She unfastened the long zip, slid the dress from her shoulders and let it pool round her feet.

'Tell me,' she said. 'If we'd been married, would you have degraded me like this?'

'And if we'd been on our honeymoon, Cressida *mou*, would you have expected either of us to remain fully clothed for very long?'

'You,' she said bitterly, 'have an answer for everything.'

'And you, my lovely one, talk too much.' Draco leaned back, watching her through half-closed eyes. 'Now take off the rest—but slowly.'

They lay together on the thick rug in front of the fireplace, his hands making a long, lingering voyage of rediscovery.

This time, she thought fiercely, she wouldn't let it happen. She wouldn't become some mindless—thing, subject to his every sexual whim. She had a will of her own and she would use it.

But it wasn't easy. Not when he was kissing her slowly and deeply, his tongue a flame against her own. Not when her breasts were in his hands and the tight buds of her nipples were unfurling slowly under his caress. Or when he was stroking her flanks, cupping the roundness of her buttocks in his palms.

And not when she needed him so desperately, so crazily, to touch her—there—at the very core of her womanhood.

He whispered against her lips. 'This time you have to ask, *agapi mou*. You have to tell me what you want.'

Her voice cracked. 'Draco—please…'

'Not good enough, my sweet one. Is it this?' He kissed her breasts, taking each soft, scented mound into his mouth in turn.

'Yes,' she said. 'No. Oh, God…'

'Or this?' His fingertips brushed her intimately, as lightly as a butterfly kiss and as fleeting.

Her only answer was a soft, involuntary whimper of yearning.

'Or even—this?' His voice sank to a whisper as he bent his head and his mouth found her.

She cried out, and for a moment her body went rigid, all her inhibitions rearing up in shock.

But her one prim attempt to push him away was unavailing. He simply captured her wrists in one strong hand and did exactly as he wanted.

Which, Cressy realised, as her whole body began to shake in sudden wanton delight, was exactly what she wanted too.

The last vestiges of control were dissolving under the warm, subtle flicker of his tongue. She was going wild, her head twisting from side to side, the breath bursting hoarsely from her lungs. Pleasure was filling her like a dark flame, driving her to the limits of her endurance. And beyond.

Her whole being seemed to splinter in a rapture so intense she thought she might die.

As awareness slowly returned, she realised she was kissing him, her parted lips clinging to his in abandoned greed. She had marked him too, she saw. There were small crescents on the smooth skin of his shoulders that her nails had scored in those final fainting seconds.

She felt bewildered—and ashamed that her resistance could be so easily and swiftly destroyed. And she was angry, too, because she didn't want to be Draco's creature, locked into this—sexual thrall.

He raised his head and looked down at her.

He said, his voice slurred, 'I couldn't concentrate at my meeting for thinking of your loveliness—your sweetness. I should be at a dinner tonight with a group of other bankers, but I had to find you—to be with you...'

She turned her head, avoiding his gaze. 'Am I supposed to be grateful?'

'No,' he said with sudden harshness. 'Just willing.'

He lifted her hips towards him, and smoothly and expertly joined his body to hers.

She could not fight him physically—she was no match for his hard, virile muscularity—but she could close her mind against him. Force herself to lie passive and unresponsive beneath him—refuse herself the delicious agony of consummation that his powerful body was offering her once more. That, she discovered with shock, her own sated flesh was incredibly, impossibly eager to accept.

And Draco knew what she was doing. Because he too was holding back, deliberately tempting her to abandon her self-denial and join him on the path to their mutual delight.

His mouth touched hers, softly, coaxingly, then brushed her closed eyelids. His lips tugged at the lobe of her ear and explored the vulnerable pulse in her throat. He whispered her name almost pleadingly against her breast.

And, in spite of everything, her iron resolve was beginning to falter, her aroused body making demands she could no longer ignore.

But Draco's patience had cracked too. He was no longer teasing, or even very gentle. Instead, he was driving himself with a kind of grim determination towards his own climax.

At its height, he cried out something in his own language, his voice harsh, almost broken.

When it was over, he rolled away from her and lay, one arm covering his eyes, as his rasping breath slowly returned to normal.

Cressy sat up slowly, pushing her hair from her eyes. She supposed she had scored a small victory, but it seemed a barren, sterile thing, especially when her newly awakened body was aching for the fulfilment she'd spurned.

She felt cold, and a little frightened. She didn't dare look at him, or say anything, even when, a long time later, he got to his feet and walked to the sofa and his discarded clothing. A brooding silence enclosed them both.

At last he said, 'You made me use you. Why?'

She said, 'I assumed you wished to be repaid for my

father's medical bills. You can't always choose the currency.'

He whispered something under his breath, and the controlled violence of it made her flinch. He picked up her dress and tossed it to her. 'Cover yourself.'

She slipped it over her head, but didn't fasten it. She didn't trust her shaking hands to deal with the zip.

He was fully dressed when he spoke again, his tone clipped, remote. 'You will find food in the kitchen. I brought a hamper from London. There is chicken, and champagne and peaches.'

She ran her tongue across her dry lips. 'Aren't you hungry?'

'I find I do not wish to eat with you,' he returned curtly. 'Besides, I think it best if I go before I do something I shall regret.'

He walked to the door and she followed him, barefoot, holding the slipping dress against her.

She said, her voice faltering a little, 'Did you drive yourself here? I didn't see another car.'

'I parked at the back of the house. The housekeeper directed me.'

'In my father's place?' Her voice rose. 'Oh, God, how could she do such a thing?'

'Because, unlike you, Cressida *mou*, she seems able to accept that I am the master here now.'

Hurt exploded inside her, and an odd sense of desolation.

She said thickly, 'Damn you,' and swung back her hand. She wanted to hit him—to drive the expression of cold mockery from his face.

But he was too quick for her, grabbing her wrist with hard fingers, shaking her slightly, so that the damned dress slid off her shoulders again, baring her to the waist.

She saw his face change, become starkly intent. He said softly, 'There is only one way to deal with a woman like you.'

He swung her round so that her back, suddenly, was against the closed door. She tried to cover her breasts with her hands, but his fingers closed round her wrists, lifting them above her head and holding them there.

He said, 'It is a little late for such modesty. Rage suits you better.'

She said breathlessly, 'Let me go—you bastard...'

'When *I* choose,' he said. 'Not you.'

She heard her dress tear as it fell to the floor. He took her quickly, his anger meeting hers in an explosive fusion that stunned the senses.

She thought, This is an outrage... And then she stopped thinking altogether.

Because his hands were under her thighs, lifting her so that she had to clamp her legs round his waist, join the driving rhythm of his possession.

His mouth was crushing hers passionately, drinking the salty, angry tears from her lips. She was moaning in her throat, gasping for breath, dizzy and drowning in the merciless forces he had released in her.

She tried to push him away, but it was already too late. Deep within her she could feel the first harsh tremors of her approaching climax. As the pulsations overwhelmed her, tore through her, she sobbed her release against his lips, then hung in his arms, limp as a rag doll, incapable of speech, hardly able to think.

Draco stepped back from the door and carried her across the room, dropping her almost negligently on to the sofa.

Cressy lay, staring up at him, her face hectically flushed, her hair wildly dishevelled and her eyes wide and enormous.

His smile was mocking as he casually fastened his clothing. He reached into the inside pocket of his jacket for his wallet.

A shower of fifty-pound notes fluttered down on her.

He said softly, 'I think I have ruined your dress, *agapi mou*, so buy yourself a new one. Something that does not make you look as if you are in mourning for your virginity, hmm?'

He paused. 'And do not ever try to reject me again.'

She wanted to reach out to him, to say his name, to ask him to stay with her, but she was too shattered by the impact of the last few minutes to be able to move or formulate coherent words.

She could only watch helplessly as he turned and walked to the door, where he paused.

'And do not wait for me to apologise,' he flung back at her. 'Because I find, after all, I do not regret a thing.' And he went out, slamming the door behind him.

CHAPTER NINE

'I'M GOING to hire a detective,' said James Fielding. 'Someone who knows what he's doing. He'll find her— persuade her to come home. Of course it will cost a great deal of money, but that's not a problem. It's time I was back in the workplace, anyway. I was a damned fool to be talked into early retirement.'

There was an awkward silence. Cressy saw the swift, worried glance exchanged by her aunt and uncle, and looked down at her hands gripped together in her lap.

Every day it was the same, she thought wearily. Schemes to make new fortunes. Plans to win Eloise back. Her father could talk of nothing else. He seemed to have lost all touch with reality.

His financial difficulties—the fact that the house no longer belonged to him—were simply brushed aside as temporary difficulties.

But then who am I to criticise? she wondered. With the nightmare I've created for myself?

It had been a week since Draco had slammed out, and since then she hadn't heard a word from him.

And she was scared.

After he'd gone, she'd lain on the sofa for a long time, limbless, weightless in the aftermath of that raw, savage ecstasy. She'd never dreamed she was capable of such a primitive intensity of feeling. Was stunned by her capacity for passion.

It was as if she'd lived her life only knowing half of herself.

133

When she'd been able to move again, and think, she had gone up to her room, showered, and changed into jeans and a thin sweater. She had burned the torn dress, along with the money, in the kitchen range, and had thrown away the food and wine. She'd felt too numb to eat. Besides, it had all been too reminiscent of the picnics they'd shared on Myros, and she hadn't been able to bear to remember the uncomplicated happiness of those days.

Days, she'd thought, when I was falling in love...

And could have wept for the innocence and tenderness of that lost time.

She had recalled the way his arm had held her, fitting her to the curve of his body. The beat of his heart under her cheek. How he'd smiled at her. The reined-back hunger in his eyes. The huskiness in his voice when he'd asked her to marry him.

Everything, she'd thought bleakly, that she'd thrown away with both hands.

And no amount of sex, however mind-blowing, would ever make up for that.

By the time Berry had returned she'd managed to regain some kind of composure. She'd spent the evening in the study, working on her computer, tying up some loose ends from work and listening to music.

'Has your visitor gone, Miss Cressy?' Berry looked around her as if she might find him hiding in a corner. 'You could have knocked me down with a feather when he told me he was the new owner and showed me the papers.' She lowered her voice. 'I didn't really want to leave him here, but he was so persuasive.' She shook her head. 'Not an easy gentleman to say no to. But did I do the right thing?'

'Yes, of course.' Cressy smiled at her with a tranquillity she was far from feeling. 'I suppose he thought it was time he saw what he was getting for his money.'

'And he told me Mr Fielding will be renting the house from him and we won't have to move out. Oh, that's such a relief, Miss Cressy. I've been so worried.'

So have I, Cressy thought bleakly. And my worries aren't over yet.

As each long day passed, she felt as if she was living on a knife-edge, waiting for the phone to ring. Scanning her e-mail box for messages.

But the nights were even worse. She lay awake for hours, staring into the darkness, her body aching for him—longing for him. She felt bereft—like a child crying unheard for comfort.

Perhaps he'd decided to cut his losses and shut her out of his life altogether. That was the thought that tortured her every waking moment.

She told herself that she was concerned for her father. Because if Draco had really decided to finish their relationship, it did not follow that he would write off her father's debts.

But in her heart she knew it would never be as simple as that. That she was using her father's problems as a barrier—as self-protection against a hurt that might tear her in pieces. Against feelings she dared not examine too closely in case they destroyed her.

'Cressy, dear.' Her aunt's voice reached her from some far distance. 'I think it's time we went, and let James rest.'

'Yes, of course.' She rose, reaching for her bag, aware that Lady Kenny was watching her with a faint frown.

'Coffee, I think,' Sir Robert said when they were in the corridor.

In the hospital cafeteria, he joined the queue at the counter while Cressy and Barbara Kenny found a corner table.

'It doesn't get any better, does it?' Lady Kenny said abruptly. 'Poor James is like a dog with a bone. He won't let go.'

Cressy shook her head. 'And he gets so agitated when he talks about her. I know it's not good for him. What he'll be like when he gets home...'

'I wonder if that's such a good thing.' Her aunt played with her wedding ring. 'Whether he wouldn't be better living somewhere with no memories. But he'll have the nurse to keep an eye on him, and dear Berry, so we must hope for the best.' She gave Cressy a searching glance. 'Now tell me about this new job of yours.'

'There's nothing to tell,' Cressy hedged. 'I'm not even sure it's happening.'

'I gather it's connected with the Standard Trust Bank,' Lady Kenny went on, as if she hadn't spoken. 'And that the head of the bank—some Greek tycoon— has made himself personally responsible for your father's debts. Isn't that a little unusual?'

Cressy shrugged. 'I suppose so. I haven't really thought about it.'

'Even when he insisted on conducting the negotiations with you personally?' Her aunt's tone was acerbic. 'And when you'd only just come back from Greece?' She gave an exasperated sigh. 'Cressy, I'm not a fool. Are you involved with this man?'

Cressy bit her lip. 'Not in the way that you think, Aunt Bar.'

Which was no more than the truth, she thought unhappily. No one would believe the complexities of her relationship with Draco.

'I have a short-term contract,' she continued, 'which necessitates my working abroad. After what he's done for Dad, I could hardly refuse. And I can look after myself,' she added, infusing her tone with brightness.

Lady Kenny snorted. 'Oh, really? Have you looked in a mirror lately? You're all eyes and cheekbones.' She leaned forward. 'Darling, men like Draco Viannis are not philanthropists. You don't know what you're getting yourself into. Your uncle and I are both worried sick. And if your father would come down to earth for a few minutes, I know he'd put a stop to it.'

'It's for three months,' Cressy said quietly. 'If I go at all.' She swallowed. 'Mr Viannis may be having second thoughts.'

'I can't vouch for this coffee.' Sir Robert deposited a tray on the table and sat down, fixing his niece with a penetrating look. 'Now then, Cressy, I want a word about this Viannis chap. Are you sure you know what you're doing?'

They were both so kind, Cressy thought as she drove home later, and so anxious about her. And she knew she'd done nothing to set their minds at rest.

But what could she say—what reassurance could she possibly give? Especially when she herself felt as if she was operating in some kind of vacuum.

There was a strange car, large, powerful and glossy, parked in front of the house, and Berry was waiting to open the door for her.

'You've a visitor, Miss Cressy. I've shown him into the drawing room.'

Cressy's heart thudded, and her throat tightened painfully as she walked towards the drawing room. Ever since her last encounter with Draco she hadn't been inside the room, unsure if she could handle the memories it would evoke. In fact, she'd made a point of using her father's study instead.

Now she had to face him there. Brave whatever he had to tell her.

Swallowing, she twisted the handle and went in.

The anticlimax when she found herself confronted by a stranger was almost ludicrous.

Except that she did know him, she realised after a stunned moment. It was Paul Nixon, who worked as Draco's PA. She'd seen him briefly in London.

She felt sick. Draco wasn't even going to break their agreement in person.

'Miss Fielding. I'm sorry I didn't make an appointment, but Mr Viannis called from New York last night to say he'll be returning to Myros next week and wishes you to meet him there. And that doesn't leave much time.'

She felt as if she'd been reprieved from a death sentence, and was ashamed of the relief and joy that flooded through her.

She said quietly, 'I understand. Won't you sit down? Can I offer you some tea or coffee?'

'Your housekeeper already did that, ma'am.' He delved into a briefcase. 'I have a file here, with your itinerary. You'll fly first class to Athens, and transfer to Myros by helicopter. Also details of the personal allowance that you'll receive while you remain Mr Viannis's—companion, and the final settlement he is prepared to make.'

Caught on the raw, Cressy took the folder he handed her.

'What a lot of paperwork,' she said coolly, hiding her hurt. 'All to get a man into bed with a woman.'

Paul Nixon's solemn face reddened uncomfortably and he gave Cressy an austere look. 'The details of Mr Viannis's private life are no business of mine, Miss Fielding. I'm just here to do a job.'

'You do it well,' she said. 'But I'm sure you've had plenty of practice.'

He looked more po-faced than ever. 'You'll also be requested to sign a contract of confidentiality,' he went on. 'Guaranteeing that no details of your time with Mr Viannis will ever be made public.'

'In case I write a kiss-and-tell story for the tabloids?' Cressy asked with disbelief. 'My God, I'm the last person in the world who'd want to go public.'

'I'm sure that's how you feel now, ma'am. But things can change, and Mr Viannis would not wish any future marriage he might contract to be compromised by unwelcome revelations.'

She felt as if she'd been punched in the stomach, but she recovered and managed a taut smile. 'In other words, hell hath no fury, Mr Nixon. Tell your boss I'll sign his guarantee.'

She took the pen he handed her, and wrote her name where indicated.

Then she showed him to the door, wished him a pleasant drive back to London, and returned to the drawing room.

The folder was lying on the coffee table. The next three months of her life all spelled out for her in clauses, sub-clauses and settlements.

She picked it up, weighed it speculatively for a moment, then, with a small choking cry, threw it across the room as hard as she could. It hit the wall and fell, disgorging its contents on to the carpet.

And then she burst into tears.

Cressy finished rubbing sun screen on to her legs, and put the cap back on the bottle.

It would be tempting, she thought with detachment, to allow Draco to arrive and find her burned to a crisp, and consequently unavailable, but she could not risk the damage to her skin.

The sky above Myros was cloudlessly blue, the sun relentlessly hot, and the swimming pool beside her deliciously cool. If only she could relax and enjoy it...

But that was impossible.

She found herself stealing another glance at her watch, and swore under her breath. He would be here only too soon. She didn't have to mark the passage of every minute until then.

She'd arrived the previous day, leaving rain and a chill, unseasonal breeze in England.

Her father, immersed in the letters he was writing to various companies offering his services as a consultant, had wished her an almost casual goodbye.

At one time she would have been wounded by his self-absorption. Now she had her own immediate problems to deal with.

The resident nurse, a Miss Clayton, was a kind, sensible woman, and Cressy had liked her at once. But it was clear she had a struggle on her hands to induce James Fielding to rest.

'It's not just a question of medication,' she'd told Cressy as they shook hands. 'He needs to relax more.'

Don't we all? thought Cressy, with irony, reaching for the iced lemonade on the table beside her. She might be in the equivalent of Eden, but she was like a cat on hot bricks just the same.

However disapproving Mr Nixon might be, there had been nothing wrong with his travel arrangements. It had been VIP treatment all the way.

The villa was just as beautiful as she'd imagined, with large airy rooms and exquisitely tiled floors, and a magical view of the sea from every window. And although it was luxurious, it wasn't stridently so. The furniture tended to be on the heavy, old-fashioned side, suggesting it had been passed down over several generations, and Cressy found it charming.

And the service was faultless, she thought. Courteous and unobtrusive.

If Vassilis, Draco's elderly major-domo, had reservations about his employer's choice of guest, he gave no sign of it.

She knew now what building work Draco had found it necessary to supervise, because she was living in it.

It was a guest bungalow, completely separate from the villa itself, with its own garden and pool, tucked away in a corner of the grounds.

It had a large living room, where her meals were served, a bathroom, with a big sunken tub as well as a conventional shower, and a huge bedroom, with walls painted in pale gold and a king-size bed with an ivory cover, draped in matching filmy curtains.

The perfect love nest, she'd thought, lips twisting, as Vassilis had shown her round it. All that was lacking was the perfect love.

But at least she was the first one to stay there. She hadn't had to spend her first sleepless night speculating on the women who'd occupied this bed before her. Her successor could worry about that.

Pain knifed at her, but she couldn't let that matter. She had to keep reminding herself of the tenuous nature of her position. Accustom herself to the idea that she had no permanent role in Draco's life.

And perhaps by the time it ended she would have learned to live with the pain.

In the distance, she heard the sound of a helicopter. She scrambled off the cushioned lounger and stood, staring upwards, her hand shading her eyes, her heart thumping against her ribcage.

It came in low enough for her to be aware of a figure—a face looking down at her—then descended towards the pad on the far side of the main house.

She took a deep, steadying breath, and thought, He's here.

And now, as Vassilis had tactfully indicated, she must wait to be summoned.

Fright and excitement warred inside her for control. After a moment, she resumed her place on the lounger. She didn't want to be found standing beside the pool as if she was planning to drown herself.

She picked up the magazine she'd been glancing through and tried to concentrate on it as the minutes dragged by.

It was over an hour later when Vassilis's upright figure appeared in the gap in the high flowering hedge that divided the bungalow from the rest of the grounds.

He said in his careful English, 'Mr Viannis presents his compliments to you, madam, and asks if you will dine with him this evening. He suggests ten o'clock.'

Six hours to go, Cressy thought. Draco was playing it cool. Whereas she might well become a nervous wreck.

Aloud, she said sedately, 'Please thank Mr Viannis,

and tell him I'd be delighted.' She paused. 'Am I to join him at the main house?'

'Yes, madam. I shall conduct you there.' He made her a small half-bow, and turned away.

Well, what had she expected? she asked herself with self-derision as she went back to her magazine. That Draco was going to rush to her side and smother her with kisses?

She was being taught her place, she thought, in one unequivocal lesson.

But, she told herself forlornly, she would have preferred the kisses.

She spent a lot of time that evening deciding what to wear. In the end she chose a cream silk shift, with bootlace straps and a deeply slashed neckline that skimmed the inner curves of her breasts. The minimum of underwear and a pair of cream strappy sandals with high heels completed the outfit.

Dressing the part, she thought, as she brushed her hair to fall in a silky curtain on her shoulders. But wasn't that what he was paying for?

She noticed that Vassilis kept his eyes discreetly lowered when he came to collect her.

It was a warm, sultry night, and the cicadas were busy as she walked through the garden. There were lights on inside the villa, and on the terrace which surrounded it.

One massive pair of sliding glass doors stood open, leading, she knew, to the *saloni*, and Vassilis paused outside, indicating politely that she should precede him into the lamplit room.

Lifting her chin, she obeyed, aware of him closing the doors behind her. Shutting her in.

He was standing at a side table, pouring himself a

drink. He was wearing jeans, and a dark polo shirt, unbuttoned to reveal the shadowing of hair on his chest, and for a brief moment her heart lifted as she saw the lover she'd first met.

Then he turned and studied her, the firm mouth unsmiling, and she knew she was mistaken.

He said softly, 'So, here you are.'

'As you see,' she said, masking her real emotions with flippancy. 'Stripped, bathed, and brought to your tent.'

His tone was flat. 'You are not amusing.' He pointed to the cloudy liquid in his glass. 'I am drinking ouzo. May I get you some?'

'I'd prefer plain water.'

He gave her a cynical look. 'How abstemious of you, *agapi mou*,' he drawled. 'You don't feel that alcohol might dull the edge of your coming ordeal?'

'Is that how you regard it?'

Draco shrugged. 'I want you very badly.' The dark eyes met hers in a frankly sensual challenge. 'And I am not in the mood to make allowances.'

Her throat tightened. She was aware that her skin was tingling, her entire body stirring with irresistible excitement under its thin silken covering.

Faint colour rose in her face, but she didn't look away.

She said, 'I'll take the risk.'

He lifted a sceptical brow, then turned back to the table, dropping ice cubes into a tumbler and filling it with water.

When he came across to give her the glass, Cressy felt her pulses surge. She thought that he would touch her, run his fingers down her bare arm, take her hand, kiss her mouth.

But he stepped back, lifting his own glass in a mocking salute. 'To courage, *pethi mou*,' he said, and drank.

They had dinner on the terrace, the table lit by glass-shaded candles. Vassilis brought them a light creamy soup, delicately flavoured with lemon, then fish baked with herbs, served with tiny potatoes and a green salad.

The food was delicious but Cressy had to force herself to eat. She was too aware of the shadowed face of the man who sat opposite her. Conscious of the caress of his dark eyes on her lips, her shoulders, her breasts. And she felt deep within her the slow ache of anticipation.

The silence between them was electric—alive with tension. As if, she thought, a storm was brewing.

She said, trying to introduce an element of normality, 'How was New York?'

'Like an oven. I prefer to go there in the fall.'

'Was your trip successful?'

'Thank you, yes.' There was faint amusement in his voice.

'And was the flight back tiring?'

'Yes, but I have amazing powers of recovery.' He was grinning openly now, and she felt herself blush.

After a pause, he said, 'You sound as if you have been taking lessons.'

'In what?' She sent him a puzzled look.

'Polite conversation for difficult situations,' he said silkily. 'And don't glare at me like that, or Vassilis will think we have quarrelled,' he added as the older man came soft-footed along the terrace.

He brought dessert—a bowl of fresh peaches and glossy black grapes—and when he had filled tiny cups with strong, bitter coffee, he discreetly vanished.

Cressy said, constrainedly, 'He's been very kind.'

His mouth twisted. 'He is paid to be.'

She drank some of the smoky brew. 'Is that what I'm paid for, too?'

He said harshly, 'No, it is not kindness I want from you. And you know it.'

'Then what?'

His smile was crooked. 'For tonight, *agapi mou*, I want you naked in my arms, and I cannot wait any longer. Come with me now.'

Her high heels made it difficult for her to keep up with his stride as they went through the moonlit garden, so she kicked off her sandals and ran beside him, barefoot.

Instantly he lifted her into his arms and carried her the rest of the way. As they reached the bungalow he stopped and kissed her, his mouth fierce and hungry, and she put her arms round his neck and held him, her lips parting eagerly beneath his.

A lamp had been lit in the bedroom, the covers were turned back, and a bottle of champagne on ice had been placed on the night table.

She thought, The stage is set, and wished it hadn't been. That no outsider had intruded on their first night together.

And then Draco kissed her again, and she forgot everything as her need for him surged through her.

He undid the single button which held her dress at the back, and it slid down her body to the floor. He knelt, stripping off her remaining covering, then buried his face against the slight concavity of her abdomen.

He whispered, 'I have dreamed of this, Cressida *mou*, of the scent of your skin—the taste…'

He picked her up and put her on the bed, shrugging

off his own clothes as he came down beside her. He kissed her mouth, and her breasts, then entered her, and she was so very ready, her body opening sweetly for him.

His taking was strong and powerful, and she gave without reserve, glorying in the muscled heat that filled her, taking him deeper and deeper, her mouth soft and moist under his, her fingers grazing his spine.

The final dark rapture took them both unawares. She cried out against his mouth, startled by the force that convulsed her, and heard his deep groan of pleasure in reply.

There were tears on her face, and his eyelashes were wet, but his lips were warm and sure against hers, and the fingers that stroked her body were endlessly tender.

And it was the most natural thing in the world to fold herself into the strong curve of his body and sleep.

But some time later, when she stirred drowsily and reached out to him, the place beside her was empty. And cold, too, as if he'd been gone a long time.

She had expected him to be there. Had counted on waking to the new day in his arms. Instead, loneliness was an icy hand at her throat.

She could just catch the fragrance of the cologne he used on his pillow. It was all that was left of him in the moonlit room, so she pulled the pillow into her arms and held it tightly, breathing the scent of him as she waited for the dawn alone.

CHAPTER TEN

CRESSY turned at the end of the pool, and cut back through the turquoise water with her clean, easy stroke. She'd already completed ten lengths, hoping that strenuous exercise would clear her mind and calm the agony of emotional confusion raging inside her.

Last night when she made love with Draco she had felt that it wasn't just a mating of their bodies, but their spirits too. And she was sure he'd been as moved by their attunement as she had.

She'd expected—she'd needed to sleep in his arms, and wake to feel his mouth warm and drowsy against hers. She'd hoped he would feel the same.

But he'd walked away. And realising that, for him, it had just been another sexual encounter—enjoyable, but soon forgotten—had been a cruel lesson to learn.

Vassilis had brought her breakfast as usual to the little vine-covered pergola, and it had taken all her resolve not to ask where Draco was, if he would be joining her. Or even if he'd sent her a message...

Well, she knew the answer to that too. Because he had not.

Underlining yet again that she had no real importance in his life, apart from the fact that he found her body desirable.

And perhaps she'd needed that kind of reminder, or she might have allowed the euphoria of the previous night to betray her into saying something really stupid. Something he would not want to hear.

148

She reached the other end of the pool and paused, shaking the drops of water from her face. As she did so she felt strong hands slide under her arms and draw her bodily up out of the water.

'*Kalimera*,' Draco said, as he set her down on the tiled surround. He was wearing elegant pale grey pants, and a white shirt, open at the neck.

'I—I didn't know you were there.' She made a business of wringing the excess water from her hair.

'I have been watching you,' he said. 'Tell me, *pethi mou*, are you training for the next Olympic Games?'

She shrugged. 'Swimming is good exercise.'

He said softly, 'I know another,' and pulled her towards him.

She hung back. 'I'm soaking. Your clothes will be ruined.'

'Then I'll take them off,' he said, and began to unbutton his shirt.

'Your staff...'

'Know better than to interrupt us. Besides, the maids have finished.'

She knew that. She had seen them leave while she was having breakfast, carrying the unwanted champagne and talking and giggling together. No doubt mulling over the fact that Kyrios Draco had found nothing to celebrate during his night with his *anglitha*. She'd felt stung, and his casual reference galled her all the more.

She said breathlessly, 'Is this what you expect? That I just—perform to order at any hour of the day and night?'

His shirt went to join the grey suit jacket and silk tie which, together with a briefcase, were already lying on one of the sun loungers.

He said, 'I was not aware, *agapi mou*, that I had asked you to perform at all.' He unzipped his trousers and stepped out of them, revealing brief black swimming trunks.

He regarded her bleakly. 'I have been in a meeting on Alakos since early morning. Perhaps I should have stayed there rather than hurry back to be with you. Or maybe you would prefer me to return to the main house for my swim?'

She said, stumbling a little, 'No—stay—please.' She looked at him appealingly. 'Draco, try to understand. This—isn't easy for me.'

His voice was cold. 'It was not intended to be.' He walked to the edge of the pool and dived in.

Cressy towelled herself down, then retired rather miserably to her lounger under the sun umbrella. Somehow he'd managed to wrongfoot her again, she thought.

When Draco eventually emerged from the pool, he dried himself quickly, then stretched out on one of the spare loungers a few feet away. He did not speak, or look at her, but busied himself with some papers he took from his briefcase.

With a smothered sigh, Cressy reached for the sun screen and began to apply it to her legs, aware that Draco's eyes had flickered briefly in her direction.

Making her wonder at the same time exactly how much of his attention it would be possible to attract.

He had put her firmly in her place, but how strong was his resolution to keep her at a distance?

She spent a long time smoothing on the lotion, lifting each slender leg in turn and running her hands slowly over her calves and up to her thighs, aware that his gaze was straying for longer and longer periods in her direction.

When she'd finished her legs, she began on her abdomen, using just her fingertips and upward circular movements until her bikini bra got in the way.

She unhooked it, and dropped it to the tiles, and began gently and very delicately to rub sun screen on to her breasts, paying particular attention to her nipples.

A lightning glance from under her lashes at Draco revealed that he'd abandoned all pretence of studying his papers, and instead was lying on his side, propped up on one elbow, watching her with undisguised appreciation.

He said softly, 'For a lady who does not perform, you're putting on quite a show, Cressida *mou*.'

She said, 'I don't want to burn…'

'No,' he said. 'You wish me to do so, instead.'

She gave him a small, cool smile, lifting her hands to push her hair back from her face, so that her breasts tilted upward in deliberate provocation.

'I thought you liked to look at me.'

'I do. You are very lovely. That is why I had your bedroom designed in gold and ivory—so that it would match your hair and your skin. Even if, as I thought then, I could only enjoy the picture you'd make in my imagination. Or on our wedding night,' he added almost casually.

She winced inwardly. She said, 'I hope I didn't disappoint you.'

'Not physically, *agapi mou*. Your body is all that a man could dream of.' His smile did not reach his eyes.

'But?' Cressy lifted her chin. 'Isn't that what you were going to say?'

He said, 'I was going to quote from your Shakespeare's *Troilus and Cressida*—when Troilus realises he has been betrayed.' His voice was quiet, almost reflective. '"If beauty have a soul, this is not she".'

Colour flared in her face. She reached for her discarded towel and pulled it across her body.

She said quietly, 'That's—cruel...'

'Perhaps,' he said. 'I am not in the mood for kindness.' He stood up, stretching indolently, then picked up his clothes.

He said, 'However, I'm hungry and I'm tired. I'm going up to the house to have some food, and then sleep for an hour or two. *Herete*, Cressida *mou*.'

She said quickly, before her courage deserted her, 'You don't have to go. You could have lunch here, and then we could—sleep together—in the beautiful room you made for me.'

There was a silence, then Draco shrugged, his eyes hard. 'I fear that is not possible. You see, to me, sleep is the ultimate surrender between a man and a woman. It signifies trust—mutual dependence, commitment. And I swore a long time ago that it was an intimacy I would only share with my wife.'

She hadn't known it was possible to hurt so much. She said, 'I see,' and was astonished that her voice didn't break.

His smile grazed her skin. 'But if you feel inclined to "perform" again at some time, you have only to let me know. I will be delighted to join you.'

And he walked away, leaving her staring after him, her eyes blurred with tears.

I suppose, Cressy told herself drearily, that this is what's known as stalemate.

She'd found her way out of the garden and was standing on the headland itself, staring out to sea, her hair whipping about her face.

The wind had risen in the night, and below her the water had been stirred into little foam-capped waves.

There was no way down to the shore that she could see, but it was good just to get away from the immediate vicinity of the bungalow.

There were times, she thought restively, when she felt as if she was in solitary confinement.

She hadn't seen Draco for nearly a week now. True, he wasn't always there. The helicopter had been buzzing backwards and forwards regularly. But when he was at home he made no attempt to seek her company.

And pride, as well as fear of another rejection, prevented her from asking him to come to her.

'Kyria Fielding.' She looked round to see Vassilis hurrying towards her. 'I could not find you. I was concerned.'

'Did you think I'd run away again—or that I was going to throw myself over?' Cressy asked drily.

'That is not a subject about which to make jokes,' he said reprovingly, and she sighed.

'I'm sorry, Vassilis. Is there a problem?'

'I have brought your lunch, *kyria*. It will be getting cold.'

She sat, as she always did, at the small table he'd laid for her on the terrace. Her napkin was spread on her lap, and wine was poured into her glass.

The service remained impeccable, she thought, wondering if Vassilis found it strange that his employer's mistress should be spending her days and nights alone. Whatever his views, he was too well-trained to betray them.

He took the lid from a dish and served her a tiny

boned chicken stuffed with a delicately savoury rice. It was delicious, as usual, but as she ate Cressy thought with nostalgia of the meals she'd eaten at Yannis's taverna.

Instead of this evening's gourmet treat, she wondered if she could persuade Draco to take her out to eat. Spit-roasted lamb, she thought, and a Greek salad, and some rough red wine.

And maybe he would dance for her, and smile at her because he saw once more the girl he'd fallen in love with.

It was worth trying, anyway. Anything, she thought, was better than this limbo she was currently occupying.

She began to plan. She would ask Vassilis to arrange transport for her to Myros town, so that she could tell Yannis and Maria they were coming and get them to reserve the usual corner table.

She would also get her hair trimmed, she thought, combing its tangles with her fingers. She might even buy something to wear—something demure, and pretty, and very Greek.

But first she had to see Draco, and invite him formally to have dinner with her. And when he arrived at the bungalow that evening she would tell him he was driving her to Myros instead.

All she needed now was an excuse to go up to the house.

The telephone, she thought, with sudden inspiration. She could say she needed to call her family in England, which was no more than the truth. She'd rung home on her first evening, to tell them all she'd arrived safely, but she'd been reluctant to call again, in case she was faced with questions she couldn't answer.

I'll just have to risk it, she told herself.

She changed into a pair of slim-fitting white trousers, topping them with a dark blue cotton knit sweater with short sleeves and a discreet neckline.

Neat, she thought, as she brushed her hair and tied it back at the nape of her neck with a scarf, but not over-seductive.

Vassilis was clearly surprised to see her when she presented herself at the main door a few minutes later, but he nodded when she mentioned the telephone.

'I will ask for you to use the one in Kyrios Draco's study, madam. It is more private there.'

He led the way to a thick, heavily carved wooden door, and tapped. There was a moment's low-voiced conversation in Greek, then he stood back.

'Go in, madam, if you please.'

So far so good, thought Cressy, pinning on the casually pleasant smile she'd been practising.

But it wasn't Draco who rose with formal politeness as she entered, but Paul Nixon.

'Miss Fielding.' His tone held faint surprise. 'If you're looking for Draco, he's in Athens.'

Disappointment was like a slap in the face.

She said, 'I didn't realise. I didn't hear the helicopter.'

'He went very late last night,' he said. 'I guess you were asleep.' He paused. 'I understand you wish to use the phone?'

No, she thought. I want to make an assignation with my lover.

She said, 'Yes, if that's possible. I'm feeling guilty about my family.'

'And we can't have that.' There was something in his tone, as he gathered up the papers he was working on, which needled her. At the door, he paused. 'You know the code for the UK? Then I'll leave you to it.'

She spoke to her aunt first. 'Aunt Bar—how's everything going? How's Dad?'

'I'm not altogether sure,' Lady Kenny said slowly. 'Your uncle and I went to lunch there yesterday, and he seemed quiet, almost subdued. And he didn't mention Eloise once.' She sighed. 'I think he's finally coming to terms with the fact that she's never coming back.'

'But that's a good thing—isn't it?'

'We must hope so.' Her aunt paused. 'And you, Cressy—how are things with you?'

'Oh, fine,' she said brightly, crossing her fingers in the folds of her skirt. 'You don't have to worry about me.'

When she rang her home, Nurse Clayton told her that her father was proving a model patient, if a little low-spirited.

'A call from you could be just what he needs to cheer him up,' she added.

Her father's voice sounded quiet and tired. He said, 'Sid, darling, I was hoping you'd ring. I've been doing a lot of thinking, and I realise I haven't been very fair or very kind to you for a long time now.'

'Oh, Dad.' Her throat constricted. 'You don't have to say this. Not now.'

'Yes,' he said. 'I must. I don't even know how much personal responsibility you've taken for my financial mess. No one seems prepared to give me any straight answers.' He paused. 'And it matters, because you're all I've got, and you're precious. So, tell me the truth, Sid. This Viannis—is he treating you well?'

'Yes,' she said steadily. 'Yes, he is. And I'll be home very soon now. We'll talk properly then.'

'It's good to hear your voice,' he said. 'I just needed to tell you I was sorry. Bless you, Sid, and take care always.'

She replaced the receiver, frowning a little. She'd never heard him like that before, speaking as if every word was an effort.

She thought, I'll arrange with Draco to ring each day from now on.

She found Paul Nixon waiting in the big square entrance hall.

She said, 'Thank you for the use of the room. I wonder if I could put you to some more trouble.'

'You can always ask.'

It didn't sound particularly hopeful, she thought, bewildered, but she pressed on.

'I was wondering if someone could drive me to Myros town?'

'For what purpose?'

This time his curtness was undisguised.

She flushed. 'Because I haven't been outside the grounds of this villa since I got here.' She ticked her reasons off on her fingers. 'Because I need a hairdresser, and because I'd like to visit Yannis and Maria at the taverna again. I hope that's all right,' she added with a touch of sarcasm.

He said, 'I'll arrange for a beautician from the hotel to visit you here.'

She stared at him. 'I said I'd like to go out.'

'I'm afraid that's not possible, Miss Fielding. Draco wishes you to remain in the environs of the Villa Hera.'

She laughed disbelievingly. 'You mean I can't even go for a walk? But that's ridiculous.'

'This is a small island, Miss Fielding,' he said quietly. 'With traditional views and values, which Draco respects. And your status has changed since you were last here.'

She stiffened as she realised what he was implying. 'You mean Maria might not want to meet Draco's whore?'

'Precisely. Also your presence here is a matter of total discretion. Draco does not wish that compromised—largely for your own sake. One day you won't have his protection. And as his discarded mistress you'd be a fair target for the gutter press.'

There was a note almost like relish in his tone.

The breath caught in her throat. She said. 'You don't like me very much, do you?'

'I work for Draco, Miss Fielding. I don't judge how he chooses to amuse himself.'

'Really?' Cressy raised her eyebrows. 'I get the impression you've been judging me ever since I stepped out of that penthouse lift in London.'

He looked at her icily. 'Okay, Miss Fielding. You want to hear it—you'll get it. Draco and I go way back. We were at school together in the States, and at college. He was best man at my wedding, and I planned to stand up for him when he married this shy Aphrodite that he'd found on a beach. A girl he worshipped, and who loved him for himself alone. Someone he'd thought he'd never find.

'Only there was no wedding, and you know why. My wife and I were right here when he realised you'd dumped him and run.'

He drew a harsh breath. 'I had to watch my best friend go to pieces in front of me, and it wasn't pleasant. He was torn apart—going crazy. You damn near destroyed him, and if you're suffering a little in return, that's fine with me.'

He shook his head. 'I never wanted him to get involved with you again, but I guess this is his way of finally getting you out of his system, so I sure hope it works.

'And don't bother running to him to get me fired when he comes back tonight, lady,' he added curtly. 'My letter of resignation will already be on his desk.'

She made herself meet the cold accusation, the hostility in his eyes.

She said tonelessly, 'Why should you lose your job for telling the truth? I—I shan't say anything to Draco. And I hope you'll stay and go on being his friend.'

She walked past him towards the door and the sunshine beyond, then turned. Her voice trembled. 'And, for the record, you can't possibly blame me more than I do myself.'

The breeze was still strong, so she spent the remainder of the afternoon inside the bungalow, curled up in a corner of the big, deeply cushioned sofa which dominated the living area, her arms wrapped round her body in a vain attempt to stop herself shaking.

Paul Nixon's words had brought home to her as never before exactly what she'd done. She thought of Draco, scorned and humiliated, like an eagle brought low, and pain tore at her.

I'm no better than Eloise, she thought. I left, too, without considering the ruin and desolation I was leaving behind. And I did that to the man I loved, whereas I don't believe she ever cared for my father.

But her father had forgiven. Had gone on loving Eloise in spite of everything.

Which Draco had not. And once his need for revenge was satisfied, she would be out of his life for ever.

'I'd go to him on my knees,' she whispered. 'If I thought it would do any good. If he'd hold me just once more as if he was keeping me safe against the world. But it's too late.'

A short while later she heard the helicopter passing overhead. And fifteen minutes afterwards became aware of approaching footsteps striding swiftly across the terrace.

She scrambled to her feet, and waited for the door to open.

The wind had ruffled his dark hair. As she looked at him, she felt her heart contract with helpless yearning.

He said, 'Paul tells me you were asking for me.'

'Only to get your permission to telephone England.'

He frowned slightly. 'Naturally, you have it. You do not need to ask. I will arrange to have a phone installed here for your personal use.'

'That's kind,' she said. 'But there's no real need.'

He said quietly, 'Please allow me to do this for you.' He paused. 'Was your call satisfactory?'

'I suppose so.' It was her turn to hesitate. 'I'm worried about my father.'

'I'm sorry.'

'It's probably nothing,' she said. 'He just sounded so defeated somehow.' She sighed. 'But he called me Sid. And he hasn't done that for a very long time.'

He looked her over, smiling slowly. 'And is that who you are now?'

'Only until the sun goes down.' She met his dark gaze. 'Will you have dinner with me this evening?'

'Why, *agapi mou*?' he drawled. 'Is this your way of telling me that you're available again?'

No, she thought, it's my way of telling myself that if

a few hours of lovemaking are all I'm allowed of you, then I'll settle for that.

She shrugged, watching him through her lashes. 'Find out for yourself, *kyrie*—after dinner.'

His brows lifted in mocking acknowledgement. He walked across to her and pulled her against him, his lips exploring hers in warm, sensuous appreciation. At the same time he untied the scarf confining her hair, separating the silky strands with restless fingers and drawing them forward to frame her face.

She laughed and shook her head. 'It needs cutting.'

'I forbid it,' he said huskily. 'It would be a crime against humanity.'

He drew her down to sit beside him on the sofa. He said, 'I have to go away again tomorrow.'

'Must you?' She moved slightly so that his fingers could more easily cup her breast. 'Where this time?'

'New York.'

'I thought you didn't like it there in summer.'

'I have no choice. I have business to settle, and a possible merger to arrange.'

'Tell me about it.' She slipped a hand into the open neck of his shirt, her fingers tracing patterns among the crisp dark hair.

He shook his head. 'I never talk about deals before they are concluded.'

'My father used to say that.'

'Presumably before his business acumen deserted him.' His tone was faintly acerbic.

'It wasn't entirely his fault,' she protested. 'He was under pressure from my stepmother, and he could never refuse her anything. She helped con him out of the money, and now she's gone off with the man who ruined him, and he'd still have her back if he could.'

He gave her a cynical look. 'Love drives you crazy, *pethi mou*. Didn't you know?' He kissed her again. 'I'll go now. I need a shower and a drink before dinner, and I have some calls to make.'

'Is it always like this?' she asked. 'Phone calls and meetings, and dashing from city to city?'

'Not always.' He ran a caressing hand down her spine. 'And when I come back I shall make sure I have some free time to devote to you alone.' He paused. 'Do you miss me when I'm away?'

She wriggled away from his hand and the question at the same time. 'I've never been to New York.'

He was silent for a moment. 'I have too hectic a schedule for you to accompany me this time,' he said quietly. 'There'll be other trips.'

She put on one of her favourite dresses, a simple button-through style in dark green linen, with a square neck and a skirt that flared slightly. She brushed lustre on to her lips, and mascara on to her long lashes, and stroked scent on to her throat and breasts. Preparing herself for love, she thought, her mouth twisting sadly.

When she emerged from her bedroom, she was confronted by a procession of people with table linen, cutlery and glassware, all milling round in the living room.

She beckoned to Vassilis. 'Will you tell them all to go, please?'

'To go, madam?' He was clearly shocked. 'But we must make things ready for Kyrios Draco.'

'I can do that myself,' Cressy said briskly, ignoring his horrified expression. 'I can lay a table, arrange flowers and light candles.'

'But the *kyrie*…'

'The *kyrie* wants peace and privacy, and so do I.'

Cressy offered him a winning smile. 'Please make them understand I wish to be alone with him.'

He was clearly scandalised by such candour—the fiction that she was just another guest and this was an ordinary dinner party had to be maintained somehow—but he had the room emptied in minutes.

As she moved round the table, putting the final touches, Cressy let herself pretend that she was back in London, in her own flat, waiting for Draco to arrive. That once again they were lovers, with a wedding to plan and a future to dream about.

As it could have been, she thought. Only I was too much of a coward to take the risk.

When everything was as good as she could make it, she sat down and tried to compose herself. It was impossible that she should still feel shy with Draco, yet she did. Because in many ways he was still an enigma.

He made love to her with breathtaking skill and artistry, but that was such a minor part of his life. And the doors to the rest were closed to her.

Restlessly, she reached for the pile of magazines that Vassilis provided on an almost daily basis. They were mostly high-fashion glossies, which didn't interest her greatly, but there was the odd news magazine sometimes, reminding her that there was a real world outside Myros.

She picked up the latest edition and began to flick through the politics and reviews which made up most of its content.

She turned to the business pages and stopped, her whole body suddenly rigid, because Draco was there. And not alone. The full-length photograph of him in evening dress, taken outside some restaurant, also featured the beautiful girl clinging to his arm. She was tall and dark, with sultry eyes and a pouting mouth, and her spectacular figure was enhanced by a piece of designer glamour that had probably cost more than a thousand dollars per square centimetre.

'Draco Viannis with shipping heiress Anna Theodorous', ran the caption, and, numbly, Cressy turned to read the accompanying story.

Insiders, expecting to hear that the Ximenes Corporation's bid for the Theodorous tanker fleet has been successful, were intrigued last week by rumours of a more personal merger between the two giants.

Draco Viannis seems likely to surrender his bachelor status at last when his engagement is announced to Dimitris Theodorous's lovely twenty-year-old daughter Anna.

While boardroom negotiations were said to have temporarily stalled, the couple seemed inseparable at a series of fashionable Manhattan niteries, and a Ximenes source confirmed they were close.

Maybe all Dimitris has to do is wait for his rival to become his son-in-law.

Someone was moaning, a small, desolate sound in the stillness.

It was a moment before she realised that the noise was coming from herself, and pressed a hand to her mouth to stifle it.

She closed the magazine and thrust it back into the middle of the pile, as if she could somehow, by so doing, make it disappear altogether.

But there would be other stories in other newspapers and magazines that she would have to confront eventually. This would be a big business marriage, and it would not be celebrated quietly.

A whimper escaped her. But she couldn't let herself go to pieces.

It would be pointless anyway. He had made it coldly clear all along that he would marry eventually. She just hadn't expected it to be so soon. But it was none of her business. She'd forfeited all rights the day she'd agreed to his terms.

Nor was it any use telling herself that this was a political marriage rather than a love match. How many men with his money and power did follow their hearts, anyway? And Draco wouldn't risk being caught in that trap again.

Besides, having Anna Theodorous as a wife would be no hardship to any red-blooded man.

She'll be the one, thought Cressy, to sleep in his arms and be the mother of his children.

And I shall have to remember that every day for the rest of my life.

CHAPTER ELEVEN

'YOU are very quiet.' Draco watched her meditatively across the candlelit table.

She smiled at him. 'I thought you might like to eat in peace.'

'And I thought perhaps you were worn out by domesticity, *agapi mou*.' He indicated the table. 'Vassilis tells me you did all this yourself.'

'Yes,' Cressy said lightly. 'I'm amazing, aren't I? Imagine knowing where knives and forks go.'

His lips twitched. 'Can you cook as well? Does my chef have to worry?'

'I'm a very good cook, but I wouldn't dare invade his domain.'

How can I do this? she asked herself. How can I sit and chat about trivia when my heart is breaking?

He said softly, 'There seems no end to your talents, my beautiful one.'

She leaned back in her chair, letting her fingers play gently with the long stem of her wine glass, caressing the slender shaft with sensuous enjoyment. 'I try to please.'

Draco watched what she was doing with undisguised amusement. He said gently, 'Behave, Cressida *mou*.'

She let her lashes sweep down to veil her eyes. 'That's for wives, *kyrie*. Mistresses are allowed to do as they like. It goes with the territory.'

'You seem to know a great deal about it.'

'I've had to learn fast. After all, I don't want your successor to feel I'm lacking in any respect.'

'My successor?' His fork clattered to his plate. 'What in hell do you mean?'

She shrugged. 'Well, this certainly beats accountancy. I expect a long and lucrative career. Of course, I shall need you to introduce me to your friends when my three months is up,' she added casually.

He said with a snap, 'I'll make a note in my diary.'

'You sound put out.' Cressy raised her eyebrows. 'But I have to be practical. And I really should become more demanding too. After all, I'm still wearing my own clothes,' she added, frowning. 'Why wasn't there a wardrobe full of top designer gear waiting for me?'

'Perhaps because I felt you would almost certainly throw it in the sea,' he said.

'I wouldn't throw jewels in the sea,' she said. 'Or furs.'

'I admit I did not think of furs.' Draco picked up a peach and began to peel it. 'But the average temperature on Myros may have affected my judgement.'

'I could always save them,' she said. 'For New York in the fall.'

'But if you want jewels, you shall have them,' he went on, as if she hadn't spoken. 'Do you prefer diamonds or pearls?'

'Both,' she said.

His brows lifted. 'Take care, *pethi mou*. You may price yourself out of the market.'

'I'll be careful,' she said. 'And I'll be very selective next time, too, about my choice of benefactor.' She looked thoughtfully into space. 'A lonely widower, perhaps—whose daughter's just got married...'

'What is this nonsense?' There was no amusement in his voice now.

She shrugged. 'You'll be going on to the next lady. I'll have to go on to the next man.' She paused on the very edge of the abyss. Then jumped. 'You will introduce me to Dimitris Theodorous, won't you?'

Draco put down the knife he was using very carefully. 'What are you talking about?' His tone was ice.

'The merger,' she said. 'I've been reading all about it.'

'It's no secret,' he said. 'Ximenes has been negotiating for those tankers for a long time.'

'I wasn't,' she said, 'talking about tankers.'

'I did not think so.' The agate eyes glittered at her.

'Miss Theodorous photographs beautifully,' she went on recklessly. 'I loved her dress—what there was of it. Do tell her so.'

He leaned back in his chair. 'With pleasure,' he drawled. 'Which particular dress did you have in mind? She has so many.'

She had to guess. 'The Versace.'

He smiled reminiscently. 'Ah, yes.'

Cressy brought her fist down on the table. 'You bastard.' Her voice shook. 'You were with her every night in New York. Then you came back here—to me.'

He shrugged. 'What good is a woman in New York when I am on Myros?' His voice was silky.

'You're despicable.'

'No,' he said. 'Practical—like you.' His eyes blazed at her suddenly. 'And you forfeited the right to dictate to me about other lovers when you ran out on our wedding.'

She said fiercely, 'And you forfeited the same right when you forced me into bed with you.'

'You think I used force?' His chair grated across the tiled floor as he stood up. 'You are a child, Cressida *mou*. But perhaps it is time you learned another lesson. Perhaps I should show you what to expect when you find yourself in the bed of Dimitris Theodorous or any of his type.'

He strode round the table, and pulled her up from her chair by her wrist. She tried to struggle free and failed.

'Let go of me...'

'No,' he said. 'You obey orders, not give them.' He took hold of the neckline of the green dress and tore it apart, the strong fingers negligent.

She said breathlessly, 'Draco—what are you doing?'

He said, almost conversationally, 'When Theodorous goes cruising on his yacht, he takes three girls at a time. As soon as they get on board their clothes are removed, and they spend the rest of the voyage naked, even in front of the crew. Is that how you wish to be treated? Because I am willing.'

He picked her up and carried her into the bedroom, dropping her on the bed.

She stared up at him, trembling, as he began to unfasten his clothing.

She said, 'Draco—you're frightening me.'

'But this is only a demonstration, Cressida *mou*.' His smile seared her. 'The reality would be infinitely worse, I promise you.'

She shrank, sudden tears hot in her throat. 'Draco—no, please.'

There was an endless, terrible silence, then she heard him sigh. He sat down on the bed beside her and took her chin in his hand, making her look at him.

He said quietly, 'One night with Theodorous, *agapi*

mou, and you would never feel clean again, I promise you.'

He put her into the bed and drew the sheet gently over her.

Her clenched fist was pressed against her mouth. She said, 'What will happen to me when you're married?'

'Hush,' he said. 'Get some rest. We will talk about it when I get back from New York.'

He half rose, and she caught at his hand. 'Stay with me—please.'

He hesitated. 'For a little while, then.' He lay down beside her, on top of the covers, sliding an arm round her shoulders and drawing her against him.

'Aren't you going to undress?'

'No.'

'Don't you—want me?'

'Yes,' he said. 'But I do not trust myself with you, Cressida *mou*. Too much has happened tonight.'

'Oh.' She closed her eyes and put her head against his chest, soothed by the strong beat of his heart. When she spoke again, her voice was quiet. 'Are you leaving very early tomorrow?'

'Around five. I have a meeting in Athens before my plane leaves.'

She said, 'Can I see you off?' and felt him smile.

'You will be asleep.'

'No,' she said. 'No, I'll be there. I promise.'

His lips touched her forehead, and he began to talk to her very softly in his own language. She did not know what he was saying, but it didn't seem to matter, because his arms were holding her, and she felt so safe—so secure that her eyelids began to droop...

She awoke with a start, and lay, watching the grey light stealing through the shutters. She was alone, but then she'd expected to be. And who was to say that she might not soon be alone for the rest of her life?

She peered at her watch, and realised with shock that it was almost five a.m., that he would be leaving.

There wasn't time to dress or even get to the helicopter pad. She grabbed a thin white cotton robe and thrust her arms into the sleeves, fastening its sash as she ran. The tiles were icy under her bare feet, and the stones on the path outside were painful, but she didn't falter.

She flew down through the garden, her lungs on fire, as at last she panted out on to the chill, damp grass of the headland.

The sun was a sullen red disc on the horizon. Behind her, coming over the house, she heard the beat of the rotors, and she swung round, staring up into the sky, waving frantically, willing him to look down and see her.

The noise was earsplitting. The chopper was right overhead now, but she could see him, and knew that he saw her too as he lifted his hand in greeting.

And she put her hands to her mouth and shouted, 'I love you,' into the vibrating air, knowing as she did so that he couldn't hear her. That her words would be eaten, fragmented and thrown away by the machine that was taking him away from her.

She stood watching, and waving, until the helicopter was just a speck in the distance, then she turned and went slowly back to the bungalow.

'You do not eat enough, madam,' Vassilis said sternly. 'You will make yourself ill.'

'It's too hot to eat,' said Cressy.

The temperature had soared in the last few days, and the sea looked like glass, the horizon shrouded in a permanent haze. Even the big parasols near the pool were no defence against the sun's fierceness, and after her swim Cressy preferred to retreat to the shade of the terrace.

She wondered if it was equally warm in New York, but didn't dwell on it. What might or might not be happening on the other side of the Atlantic was a no-go area for her. It had to be if she was to retain any peace of mind.

And when he came back they would talk...

She watched as Vassilis, clucking, removed the remnants of her half-eaten lunch, then settled back in her chair. She hadn't slept well the previous night. She'd had a series of small hateful dreams which still hung over her like a pall, and made her feel restless and uneasy.

Or maybe a storm was brewing somewhere which would end this still, brazen heat.

She found herself wishing that the newly installed telephone would ring, and she'd pick up the receiver and hear Draco's voice saying *agapi mou*. But she knew she might as well cry for the moon. He'd called twice since he'd been away, each time asking briefly and politely if she was all right. She'd said, 'Yes' and 'Thank you' and that had been that.

He hadn't mentioned when he was coming back, and she hadn't dared to ask. Or if he would be alone when he came...

She heard the sound of footsteps and sat up with sudden incredulous hope, only to see Paul Nixon approaching.

Since their confrontation up at the Villa Hera she

hadn't set eyes on him, and as far as she knew he'd never come down to the bungalow before. Now he walked up to the terrace, and halted awkwardly in front of her.

He said, 'Miss Fielding—Cressida—there's been a phone call. I have some bad news for you.'

She felt sick, her eyes scanning his grave face. She said, 'It's Draco, isn't it? Something's happened—I knew it...'

'No,' he said quickly. 'No, Draco's fine. The call was from England—from your uncle. I'm afraid your father's had another heart attack.'

She scrambled to her feet. 'Oh, God—when? Is he back in hospital? I must go to him...'

He took both her hands in his, which was odd of him, when he disliked her so much.

He said, 'He's not in hospital. He was at home when it happened.'

Her voice seemed to belong to a stranger. She said, 'He didn't make it—did he?' And saw him bow his head in acquiescence.

He said, 'I've spoken to Draco, and I'm to escort you back to England for the funeral at once.'

She moved sharply. 'There's no need for that.'

'Yes, there is,' he told her firmly. 'You can't face this alone. If you'll pack what you need, I'll start making our travel arrangements.'

'I knew there was something wrong,' she said, her voice shaking. 'I—I dreamed it.'

'Can I get you something? Some brandy, maybe, or some tea if you'd prefer?'

She shook her head. 'I don't want anything. I'd just like to be on my way. My aunt will need me.'

'Yes.' He patted her shoulder clumsily. 'Miss Fielding—I'm truly sorry.'

She tried to smile. 'Just now you called me Cressida. If we're going to be travelling companions, perhaps you should stick to that.'

He nodded. 'I'll send one of the maids to help you pack.'

She stood watching him walk back up the path. She wanted to cry, but no tears would come.

She thought, It's over. It's all over. And, in spite of the intense heat, she shivered.

When she reached home the following day, her aunt and uncle were waiting for her.

'Cressy.' Lady Kenny took her in her arms. 'My poor darling. What a terrible homecoming.'

Cressy kissed her cheek. 'I think I was expecting it,' she said quietly. 'He sounded so different lately—like a shadow of himself. As if he'd given up.'

Her aunt hugged her, then turned to Paul Nixon, who was waiting in the doorway.

She held out her hand. 'I don't think we've met. I'm Barbara Kenny.'

'This is Paul,' Cressy said, offering him a strained, grateful smile. 'He's a friend of Draco's, and he made all the arrangements for me. He's been very kind. I—I couldn't have managed without him.'

'Yes,' Sir Robert said, shaking hands with him, 'Mr Viannis said he'd look after you.'

'You've spoken to Draco?' He seemed to have been in contact with everyone but herself, she thought painfully.

'I could hardly avoid it, my dear. He's in the drawing

room. Took an overnight flight from the States, I understand.'

Draco was standing by the window as she went in. He came towards her quickly, and she waited for him to enfold her in his arms, but instead he embraced her formally, with a kiss on each cheek, leaving her feeling faintly chilled.

'You are well?' The dark face was concerned.

She nodded. 'I didn't know you'd be here.'

'I thought I should come,' he said. 'For all kinds of reasons. I hope you will tell me what I can do to help.'

She thought, You're with me, and that's enough...

He stepped back. 'Now I will leave you with your family,' he added, and, making them all a slight bow, he went out.

A little later she saw him walking in the garden with Paul Nixon, both of them deep in conversation.

'I didn't expect to like him,' Barbara Kenny said abruptly. 'But I can't deny his charm. I gather he proposes to stay here, so you'd better come to us.'

Cressy smiled at her wearily. 'Aunt Bar,' she said, 'you know quite well that I've been living with him in Greece. It's a bit late to consider the conventions. Besides,' she added with a touch of constraint, 'this house does belong to him.'

'Well, yes.' Lady Kenny flushed slightly. 'But you're in mourning—he can hardly expect...'

Cressy bent her head. She said quietly, 'You don't have to worry, Aunt Bar. I don't think he's expecting anything.'

The door opened and Berry came in, pushing a trolley laden with tea things. Her eyes were red and puffy, and her mouth trembled when she saw Cressy.

'Oh, Miss Cressy, my dear. Poor Mr Fielding. It

shouldn't have happened. He should have had many more years—seen his grandchildren born.'

Cressy bit her lip, aware that Lady Kenny was staring at her in sudden horrified speculation.

She gave a slight, almost wistful shake of her head, then turned back to the housekeeper, her voice gentle. 'It's terrible for us, Berry, but I really don't think he wanted to go on living.'

'No, he didn't,' Berry said forcefully. 'Not after he got that awful letter from *her*.'

Cressy was startled. 'Did Daddy hear from Eloise?'

'Nancy—Nurse Clayton took the post into him. She wasn't to know, of course, but if I'd seen Mrs Fielding's writing I'd have held it back, that I would. Given it to Sir Robert first.'

'What did it say?'

'I don't know, Miss Cressy. Mr Fielding burnt it in an old ashtray in the study, so that no one else would see it. All he'd say was that she was never coming back. White as a sheet he was too, and looked as if he'd been crying. And he was never the same, after.'

'Whatever we all thought of Eloise,' Cressy said, 'Daddy truly loved her. And he didn't want to go on living without her.' She swallowed. 'I really think it's that simple.'

And I, she thought, as pain tore at her, I am my father's daughter.

It was a quiet funeral. None of James Fielding's former colleagues attended, but all the neighbours paid their respects, and the little church was full.

Draco stayed at Cressy's side throughout, which raised a few eyebrows, and she knew there were already various rumours spreading about his ownership of the house, but she didn't care.

Whatever anyone thought about their relationship, they were wrong, she told herself unhappily.

Apart from taking her arm in church, he hadn't touched her at all during the past difficult days.

At night, she remained in her old room, while Draco slept on the other side of the house. And he'd never given the slightest hint that he wished to change these arrangements.

She thought, It's over, and realised that when she'd thought the same words on Myros, she hadn't simply been referring to her father.

She felt sick and empty inside. Grief for James Fielding was now commingling with the agony of this other loss, draining the colour from her face and haunting her eyes.

She supposed he had already asked Anna Theodorous to marry him before he came away, but she wished he would tell her openly rather than leave her in limbo like this.

He promised he'd talk to me when he came back from New York, she told herself. And talk to me he will.

Nearly everyone who'd been to the church had come back to the house afterwards, and Cressy was ashamed at her own impatience when some of them showed a disposition to linger.

The last of them had just gone, and she was collecting the used sherry glasses in the drawing room, when Paul Nixon came in. He was carrying a large buff envelope.

He said, 'Draco's had to go back to London, Cressida, but he asked me to give you this.'

'He's gone?' She stared at him, the colour draining

from her face. She put the glasses down carefully. 'But he can't have done. And without even saying goodbye?'

Paul sighed. 'I guess he felt it was for the best.' He put the envelope in her hands and gave her a constrained smile. 'After all, you're a free woman now.'

'A free woman?' God, she thought, I sound like an echo.

He said, 'Look in your package.' He bent and gave her a quick peck on the cheek. 'Goodbye, honey, and good luck.'

When he'd gone, she tore open the envelope, letting its contents spill out on to the sofa. The first document was the deeds to the house, and there was a note from Draco attached to it which she seized upon.

> Your father's debts died with him, Cressida, and with them any obligation to me. So you are free to take up your own life again, and forget, if you can, all the unhappiness I have caused you.
>
> Perhaps we were fated to make each other unhappy, my beautiful one.
>
> I am also giving you back the house, with the hope that you will make your home there and find some true joy at last. I ask God to bless you.

She lifted the note and held it against her heart, staring silently, sightlessly into space.

Lady Kenny came in. 'Well, I have to confess, darling, I'm glad that's over.' She sat down with a heavy sigh. 'It's been such a horrible time for everyone. Your uncle thinks it would do us all good to go away for a few days, so what do you think?'

'It's a lovely idea,' Cressy said, putting all the papers

carefully back in the envelope. 'But I'm already going away.'

'You are?' Her aunt stared at her. 'But where?'

'To London first. To New York, maybe—if I have to. Or an island called Myros, Or anywhere.' She forced a smile. 'Wherever Draco is.'

'Oh, my dearest child, do you think that's wise?' Lady Kenny looked distressed. 'I know he's incredibly good-looking—and he's been amazingly sweet and thoughtful—in fact Robert really likes him—and I've grown quite attached myself, but—' She broke off. 'Where was I?'

'I think,' Cressy said gently, 'that you were about to tell me I'm making a big mistake.'

'Well, I have to think so. All that money and power. He can do exactly what he likes, and probably always has. And what if he gets tired of you, and breaks your heart?'

'That's a risk I'll just have to take.' Cressy bent and kissed her. 'Because I love him, Aunt Bar, and I always will. And I don't want to go on living without him either, whatever the terms.'

She saw her aunt's face change suddenly, and glanced round.

Draco was standing in the open doorway, his body as rigid as if he'd been turned to stone, his face bleak and strained.

Across the room, his gaze captured hers. Held it.

He said hoarsely. 'Are they true? Those things you were saying?'

She said, 'You came back...'

'I did not intend to. I wanted to release you completely. But I found I could not go. Not without a word. Or without holding you in my arms one last time.'

He walked slowly forward, halting a few feet away from her, while Lady Kenny rose quietly and tiptoed, unnoticed, from the room. 'I heard what you said, *agapi mou*. Every word. Did you mean it? Do you—can you love me?'

'Yes.' She looked at him pleadingly, her heart in her eyes. 'Draco—don't leave me, or send me away. Take me with you, please. I'll do anything you want. Be anything you want. I won't make waves. I'll live anywhere, if I can just be part of your life sometimes. And I won't be a threat to your marriage, I swear it.'

'You have been a threat to me since I first saw you peeping down at me on that beach on Myros.' He came to her, pulling her into his arms without gentleness. 'If you knew how I have longed to touch you through all these long sad days—to comfort you.'

'But you did.' She put up a hand and touched his cheek. 'You've been there for me all the time.'

'I used to come to your room,' he said. 'Sit in a chair and watch you sleep, counting how many more hours I had to spend with you. Feeling time slipping through my fingers. Telling myself that I had ruined everything, and that you would be glad to be rid of me.'

She said, 'Why didn't you wake me up—make love to me?'

'You were grieving for your father,' he said. 'I could not intrude on that.'

She bent her head. 'I think I did my grieving a long time ago. This time, I was just—letting him go.'

He said softly, 'Ah, *pethi mou...*'

He lifted her into his arms and sat down on one of the sofas, cradling her on his lap.

He said gently, 'Why did you leave me, my dear one? Why didn't you turn to me?'

She drew a deep breath. 'Because I was scared. My father's illness was an excuse to leave, not a reason. I—I didn't believe in love. I'd seen the damage it could do. Saw my father change completely when my stepmother came into his life, and that frightened me. I didn't want that to happen to me. I wanted to stay in control—not be at someone else's mercy for the rest of my life.

'When that call from England came, it seemed like a sign telling me I didn't have to change after all. That I could just go back to my old life and pretend nothing had happened. That I'd be safe that way.

'Only it was already too late.' She beat suddenly on his chest with her fists. 'Why didn't you tell me it was too late? Because you knew—didn't you?'

'Yes,' he said. 'I knew.' He was silent for a moment. 'So, I made you afraid of love.'

'I was more frightened of myself,' she said. 'Of the way you could make me feel. Although I didn't know the half of it then.'

He shook his head. 'How can you still love me, Cressida *mou*, when I've treated you so badly?'

'It could have been worse,' she said. 'You could simply have cut me out of your life.'

'That was never a possibility.' His voice was suddenly harsh. 'Even when I was hurt and angry, you were in my blood. I could not let you go. So I told myself you were just another tramp, who cared only for money and material things. And that I would have you on those terms.'

He stroked her hair back from her forehead. 'After our first time together, I was so ashamed—so angry with myself. You had been so sweet—so giving. You turned my revenge back on me, *pethi mou*—and I suffered.

'Every time I came to you it became more difficult to pretend. That's why I could never stay with you afterwards—hold you in my arms all night as I longed to do—because I knew I might break down and tell you how I truly felt. And you might not care.'

He sighed. 'And because I knew how temporary an arrangement it was. That your father might have another fatal attack at any time. And you would be free to walk away again, and this time I would have no power to bring you back.'

'You always had power over me.' She pressed a kiss to his tanned throat. 'The power of love—right from the first. Even when you offered me your bargain. I—I wanted to hate you, but I couldn't.'

'That last morning on Myros,' he said, 'you promised you would say goodbye to me, but you didn't come, although I delayed the takeoff. And then something made me look down, and you were there, waving to me, all in white, like the bride I'd dreamed of.

'And I told myself that when I came back from New York I would go on my knees to you if necessary, and beg you to forgive me—and to marry me.'

Her heart missed an incredulous, joyous beat. She said, 'I thought you were going to marry Anna Theodorous.'

'That was her father's plan, not mine. And he leaked the story to the newspapers to pressure me over the tanker deal.' His mouth tightened. 'He is a man who regards women as commodities, *agapi mou*. Even his own child.'

The hands that cupped her face were trembling suddenly. He said, 'Cressida—can you forgive me—after all that has happened between us? Will you be my wife?

She said wonderingly, 'Do you doubt it? Draco—you must know how you make me feel.'

'You do not have to love someone to like being in bed with them, *pethi mou*,' he told her quietly. 'As it was, each time we made love I could only think of how much happiness I had thrown away.'

'And I thought the same. Oh, why didn't you tell me?'

'I did tell you.' He smiled into her eyes. 'On our last night together on Myros. You must learn to speak Greek, my love, then you would know.'

She slid her arms round his neck, pressing herself against him. 'Can I have my first lesson now?'

He groaned. 'No, Cressida, because I have to find your aunt and arrange for you to stay at her house until the wedding. You see—I am belatedly trying to do the right thing,' he added wryly.

She said, 'Won't it be awkward for you to take me back to Myros as your wife? Perhaps we should leave things as they are. I mean—you don't *have* to marry me...'

He kissed her softly, and lingeringly. 'But you are so wrong, my heart. I do have to marry you, and very soon. I cannot wait any longer. Besides, Vassilis requires it. He told Paul while I was away that you did not eat because you were pining for me.'

'Oh,' she said. 'So you're marrying me just to please your staff.'

'And because I cannot go many more nights without sleep,' Draco added, straight-faced.

'And those are your only reasons?' Cressy sat up in mock outrage.

'There are others.' He pulled her back into his arms.

'Which we will discuss when we are less likely to be interrupted,' he added, his mouth softly exploring hers.

'What a pity,' she whispered against his lips. 'Because I have some wonderful memories of this room…

'But I want to make one thing clear,' she went on, when he allowed her to speak again. 'I'm staying with you, not Aunt Bar.'

'You will do as you're told, Cressida *mou*.' He sounded like the autocrat again, and she ran a loving finger across his lips.

'Then I shall sue you for breach of contract.' She smiled up at him. 'You bought me for three months. There are still two left—and I want them. I want *you*. Besides,' she added, 'if you'd really been going to marry Anna, you wouldn't have stopped making love to me. So why should you stop because you're marrying me instead?'

'I think there is something wrong with your logic,' Draco said, trying not to laugh. 'But I don't think I care. I am certainly not going to argue.'

She reached up and kissed him in turn, letting her tongue flicker softly along his lower lip. 'So will you dine with me tonight, Kyrios Draco? And after dinner will you please take me to bed and make love to me for hours?'

'I will.' His mouth took hers with a deep, sensual yearning that made her body melt against his. 'And after we have made love, Kyria Cressida, will you sleep in my arms for what is left of the night?'

She took a deep breath. 'Oh, yes, darling. Yes, I will.'

His arms tightened round her. 'Then it seems, my bride, that we have a bargain.'

'For three months?' Her smile was misty.

'No.' Draco looked deep into her eyes, shining for him with love and trust. 'For the whole of our lives, *matia mou.*'

HARLEQUIN *Presents*
Passion™

Looking for stories that **sizzle**?

Wanting a read that has a little extra **spice**?

Harlequin Presents® is thrilled to bring you romances that turn up the **heat!**

Every other month there'll be a
PRESENTS PASSION™
book by one of your favorite authors.

Don't miss
THE ARABIAN MISTRESS
by **Lynne Graham**
On-sale June 2001, Harlequin Presents® #2182

and look out for
THE HOT-BLOODED GROOM
by **Emma Darcy**
On-sale August 2001, Harlequin Presents® #2195

Pick up a **PRESENTS PASSION**™ novel—
where **seduction** is guaranteed!

Available wherever Harlequin books are sold.

HARLEQUIN®
Makes any time special ®

Harlequin truly does
make any time special. . . .
This year we are celebrating
weddings in style!

To help us celebrate, we want you to tell us how wearing the Harlequin wedding gown will make your wedding day special. As the grand prize, Harlequin will offer one lucky bride the chance to **"Walk Down the Aisle" in the Harlequin wedding gown!**

There's more...

For her honeymoon, she and her groom will spend five nights at the **Hyatt Regency Maui.** As part of this five-night honeymoon at the hotel renowned for its romantic attractions, the couple will enjoy a candlelit dinner for two in Swan Court, a sunset sail on the hotel's catamaran, and duet spa treatments.

To enter, please write, in, 250 words or less, how wearing the Harlequin wedding gown will make your wedding day special. The entry will be judged based on its emotionally compelling nature, its originality and creativity, and its sincerity. This contest is open to Canadian and U.S. residents only and to those who are 18 years of age and older. There is no purchase necessary to enter. Void where prohibited. See further contest rules attached. Please send your entry to:

Walk Down the Aisle Contest

In Canada	In U.S.A.
P.O. Box 637	P.O. Box 9076
Fort Erie, Ontario	3010 Walden Ave.
L2A 5X3	Buffalo, NY 14269-9076

You can also enter by visiting www.eHarlequin.com
Win the Harlequin wedding gown and the vacation of a lifetime!
The deadline for entries is October 1, 2001.

HARLEQUIN WALK DOWN THE AISLE TO MAUI CONTEST 1197
OFFICIAL RULES
NO PURCHASE NECESSARY TO ENTER

1. To enter, follow directions published in the offer to which you are responding. Contest begins April 2, 2001, and ends on October 1, 2001. Method of entry may vary. Mailed entries must be postmarked by October 1, 2001, and received by October 8, 2001.

2. Contest entry may be, at times, presented via the Internet, but will be restricted solely to residents of certain geographic areas that are disclosed on the Web site. To enter via the Internet, if permissible, access the Harlequin Web site (www.eHarlequin.com) and follow the directions displayed online. Online entries must be received by 11:59 p.m. E.S.T. on October 1, 2001.

   In lieu of submitting an entry online, enter by mail by hand-printing (or typing) on an 8½" x 11" plain piece of paper, your name, address (including zip code), Contest number/name and in 250 words or fewer, why winning a Harlequin wedding dress would make your wedding day special. Mail via first-class mail to: Harlequin Walk Down the Aisle Contest 1197, (in the U.S.) P.O. Box 9076, 3010 Walden Avenue, Buffalo, NY 14269-9076, (in Canada) P.O. Box 637, Fort Erie, Ontario L2A 5X3, Canada.

   Limit one entry per person, household address and e-mail address. Online and/or mailed entries received from persons residing in geographic areas in which Internet entry is not permissible will be disqualified.

3. Contests will be judged by a panel of members of the Harlequin editorial, marketing and public relations staff based on the following criteria:

   • Originality and Creativity—50%
   • Emotionally Compelling—25%
   • Sincerity—25%

   In the event of a tie, duplicate prizes will be awarded. Decisions of the judges are final.

4. All entries become the property of Torstar Corp. and will not be returned. No responsibility is assumed for lost, late, illegible, incomplete, inaccurate, nondelivered or misdirected mail or misdirected e-mail, for technical, hardware or software failures of any kind, lost or unavailable network connections, or failed, incomplete, garbled or delayed computer transmission or any human error which may occur in the receipt or processing of the entries in this Contest.

5. Contest open only to residents of the U.S. (except Puerto Rico) and Canada, who are 18 years of age or older, and is void wherever prohibited by law; all applicable laws and regulations apply. Any litigation within the Province of Quebec respecting the conduct or organization of a publicity contest may be submitted to the Régie des alcools, des courses et des jeux for a ruling. Any litigation respecting the awarding of a prize may be submitted to the Régie des alcools, des courses et des jeux only for the purpose of helping the parties reach a settlement. Employees and immediate family members of Torstar Corp. and D. L. Blair, Inc., their affiliates, subsidiaries and all other agencies, entities and persons connected with the use, marketing or conduct of this Contest are not eligible to enter. Taxes on prizes are the sole responsibility of winners. Acceptance of any prize offered constitutes permission to use winner's name, photograph or other likeness for the purposes of advertising, trade and promotion on behalf of Torstar Corp., its affiliates and subsidiaries without further compensation to the winner, unless prohibited by law.

6. Winners will be determined no later than November 15, 2001, and will be notified by mail. Winners will be required to sign and return an Affidavit of Eligibility form within 15 days after winner notification. Noncompliance within that time period may result in disqualification and an alternative winner may be selected. Winners of trip must execute a Release of Liability prior to ticketing and must possess required travel documents (e.g. passport, photo ID) where applicable. Trip must be completed by November 2002. No substitution of prize permitted by winner. Torstar Corp. and D. L. Blair, Inc., their parents, affiliates, and subsidiaries are not responsible for errors in printing or electronic presentation of Contest, entries and/or game pieces. In the event of printing or other errors which may result in unintended prize values or duplication of prizes, all affected game pieces or entries shall be null and void. If for any reason the Internet portion of the Contest is not capable of running as planned, including infection by computer virus, bugs, tampering, unauthorized intervention, fraud, technical failures, or any other causes beyond the control of Torstar Corp. which corrupt or affect the administration, secrecy, fairness, integrity or proper conduct of the Contest, Torstar Corp. reserves the right, at its sole discretion, to disqualify any individual who tampers with the entry process and to cancel, terminate, modify or suspend the Contest or the Internet portion thereof. In the event of a dispute regarding an online entry, the entry will be deemed submitted by the authorized holder of the e-mail account submitted at the time of entry. Authorized account holder is defined as the natural person who is assigned to an e-mail address by an Internet access provider, online service provider or other organization that is responsible for arranging e-mail address for the domain associated with the submitted e-mail address. **Purchase or acceptance of a product offer does not improve your chances of winning.**

7. Prizes: (1) Grand Prize—A Harlequin wedding dress (approximate retail value: $3,500) and a 5-night/6-day honeymoon trip to Maui, HI, including round-trip air transportation provided by Maui Visitors Bureau from Los Angeles International Airport (winner is responsible for transportation to and from Los Angeles International Airport) and a Harlequin Romance Package, including hotel accomodations (double occupancy) at the Hyatt Regency Maui Resort and Spa, dinner for (2) two at Swan Court, a sunset sail on Kiele V and a spa treatment for the winner (approximate retail value: $4,000); (5) Five runner-up prizes of a $1000 gift certificate to selected retail outlets to be determined by Sponsor (retail value $1000 ea.). Prizes consist of only those items listed as part of the prize. Limit one prize per person. All prizes are valued in U.S. currency.

8. For a list of winners (available after December 17, 2001) send a self-addressed, stamped envelope to: Harlequin Walk Down the Aisle Contest 1197 Winners, P.O. Box 4200 Blair, NE 68009-4200 or you may access the www.eHarlequin.com Web site through January 15, 2002.

Contest sponsored by Torstar Corp., P.O. Box 9042, Buffalo, NY 14269-9042, U.S.A.

PHWDACONT2

If you enjoyed what you just read,
then we've got an offer you can't resist!

Take 2 bestselling love stories FREE!

Plus get a FREE surprise gift!